KLOSTERHEIM;

OR,

THE MASQUE.

BY

THOMAS DE QUINCEY,

AUTHOR OF 'CONFESSIONS OF AN ENGLISH OPIUM-EATER.'

WITH A BIOGRAPHICAL PREFACE,

BY

DR. SHELTON MACKENZIE.

BOSTON:
WHITTEMORE, NILES, AND HALL.
NEW YORK: J. C. DERBY.
CINCINNATI: MOORE, WILSTACH, KEYS & CO.
M DCCC LV.

BIOGRAPHICAL NOTICE

BY

DR. SHELTON MACKENZIE.

Thomas De Quincey was born at Manchester (in England), on the 15th August, 1785. He passed the whole of his childhood, except for the few earliest weeks, in a rural retirement. The death of two of his young sisters, before he was six years old, first awakened in his mind the knowledge that mortality was the appointed fate of human beings. In his "Confessions of an English Opium-Eater," he has recorded in what manner such deprivations affected him when they occurred, and how then, sinking into his mind, they influenced it in later years. At the age of sixty, recurring to the period of his childhood, he said that if he should return thanks to Providence for all the separate blessings of his early situation, these four he would single out as chiefly worthy to be commemorated: that he lived in the country; that he lived in solitude; that his infant feelings were moulded by the gentlest of sisters, not by horrid pugilistic brothers; finally, that he and they were dutiful children of a pure, holy, and magnificent church.

His father, a Liverpool merchant of considerable wealth, was almost a stranger to him, passing the greater portion of each year in foreign climates supposed to be favorable to persons afflicted with pulmonary consumption, and rarely visiting Greenhay, (then a clear mile from the outskirts, but now a portion of the city of Manchester,) where his family resided. He returned home to die in his thirty-ninth year. This event took place in 1792, when Thomas De Quincey was only seven years old.

> "Left by his sire, too young such loss to know,
> Lord of himself — that heritage of woe."

The elder De Quincey left a widow and six children, to whom he bequeathed £30,000, yielding an annual income of £1600. At the age of twenty-one, about £5000 of this capital would constitute the fortune or portion of each child.

The elder De Quincey, his son states, was "esteemed during his life for his great integrity," and, himself an anonymous author, was "strongly attached to literary pursuits." His widow appears (as has been so frequently noticed in reference to men who have won distinction) to have possessed abilities of a superior class. De Quincey says, "My mother I may mention with honor, as still more highly gifted; for though unpretending to the name and honors of a *literary* woman, I shall presume to call her (what many literary women are not) an *intellectual* woman; and I believe that if ever her letters should be collected and published, they would be thought generally to exhibit as much strong and masculine sense, delivered in as pure 'mother English,' racy and fresh with idiomatic graces, as any in our language — hardly excepting those of Lady M. W. Montague."

During the four years next after his father's death, Thomas De Quincey and his brother (five years his senior) went to a day-school in Salford, — now an independent parliamentary borough, separated from Manchester by the small river Irwell. Here he was grounded in the classics. At the early age of eleven (as he confesses in his "Suspiria de Profundis,") he fell passionately in love with his cousin, a little girl a year younger than himself. He says that she "wore at that time upon her very lovely face the most angelic expression of character and temper I have almost ever seen." A year after (in 1796), when the family house and grounds at Greenhay were sold, for less than half what they had cost — (a few years later, this value would have been more than quadrupled), — De Quincey was removed to the grammar school of Bath, at which he speedily displayed a talent for making Latin verses, which obtained him consideration from his instructors and provoked hostility from his elder schoolmates. Subsequently he was sent to a school in Wiltshire, of which the chief recommendation lay in the religious character of its master.

There was an acquaintance of long standing between the elder De Quincey and the Earl of Altamont, an Irish peer, who was subsequently created Marquis of Sligo. This nobleman's eldest son, Lord Westport, was intimate with Thomas De Quincey, and, when at Eton, early in 1800, invited him to visit

Ireland with him in the ensuing summer and autumn. Accepting this invitation, De Quincey joined his friend at Eton, being then in his fifteenth year, and had the advantage (such as it was) of seeing and hearing Queen Charlotte and all the princesses, and even had an interview with George III., in an accidental rencontre at Frogmore — a pet residence of the Queen's — in which the king, as was his habit, asked a variety of questions, and rather annoyed the young interlocutor by supposing, from the foreign name, that his family had come over with the Huguenots at the revocation of the edict of Nantz, whereas they had been in England since the Conquest. Shortly after, Mr. De Quincey was an invited guest to one of the Queen's *fêtes* at Frogmore — a compliment with which, as a youth and an Englishman, he, naturally enough, was much pleased. In May, 1800, in company with Lord Westport, he first beheld and entered what he calls that " mighty wilderness, the city — no, not the city, but the nation — of London." They were merely passing through, but having to choose whether to visit Westminster Abbey or St. Paul's Cathedral, preferred the latter.

In his " Autobiographic Sketches," a full narrative is given of De Quincey's visit to Ireland, as Lord Westport's guest, through England and Wales to Holyhead — then as now the favorite port of communication with Ireland. The distance of sixty miles was traversed in thirty hours — steam navigation being then unknown. At this time, De Quincey wanted a few months of fifteen, but, thanks to the rank of his host, was introduced to Lord Cornwallis, the Viceroy of Ireland, as well as to Lord Clare (the Chancellor),

Lord Castlereagh, Foster (Speaker of the House of Commons), and other notorieties. Here, too, he witnessed the splendors of installing six knights (one of them being Lord Westport's father) of the Order of St. Patrick, and the not less impressive, but far more melancholy incident, of the final ratification, in the Irish House of Lords, of the Act by which the Parliament of Ireland was abolished, and the independence of a fine nation destroyed by the treachery of her own legislature. In one of his "Autobiographic Sketches," there is a graphic account of this "end of an auld sang" — to use Lord Bellhaven's plain-spoken criticism on the ratification of the Act of Union between Scotland and England. Soon after, De Quincey accompanied Lord Westport to that part of Connaught (the county of Mayo) in which the family estates chiefly lie, leisurely travelling in a series of short visits to the Irish nobility and gentry *en route*, and thus mixing with a higher class of society than school-boys of fifteen are generally in the way of associating with.

Early in November, 1800, De Quincey returned to Dublin, and after a short sojourn there — during which he fell in love with Miss Blake, a lovely Irishwoman, sister to Lord Wallscourt and to the Countess of Erroll — travelled back to England, Lord Westport returning to Eton, and De Quincey proceeding to Northamptonshire, on a visit to Lord Carbery, at which place intimation was made to him that some fixed resolution would be taken and announced to him with regard to the future disposal of his time until, two or three years later, he should be old enough to matriculate at Oxford or Cambridge. In the following year (1801), he was at Liverpool, where he became acquainted with Dr. Currie (the first biographer of Burns), Dr. Shepherd, author of a Life of Poggio Bracciolini, and William Roscoe. A little earlier, he had become known to, and intimate with, the Rev. John Clowes, who died in 1831, after having been rector of St. John's, Manchester, for more than sixty years, and, becoming imbued with Swedenborg's peculiar doctrines, had devoted a great portion of his large income to the translation and publication of his numerous works.

On his father's death, Thomas De Quincey had been left under four male guardians and his mother. One of these lived at a distance, and is described as being "more reasonable and having more knowledge of the world than the rest." Two others resigned their authority into the hands of the fourth, "a worthy man in his way, but haughty, obstinate, and intolerant of all opposition to his will." In the summer of 1802, De Quincey, who was fully competent to enter college, (he says that at thirteen he wrote Greek at ease and, at fifteen, not only composed Greek verses in lyric measures, but could converse in Greek fluently and without embarrassment, being in the daily practice of reading off the newspapers in Greek *extempore*,) applied to his guardians for permission to do so. They consented, agreeing to give him an annual allowance of £200, then universally regarded as the *minimum* for an Oxford student. But annexed to this grant was the condition that De Quincey should then make a positive and definite choice of a profession. Had he chosen the law, perhaps the next three or four years of his life should be spent, not at Oxford, as he earnestly desired, but in the chambers of a special pleader in London. He determined not to give the required pledge, and (in August, 1802), a few days before his seventeenth birth-day, finding that he had to hope for no compromise with his guardian's resolute will, eloped from school, with twelve guineas in his pocket — ten of which were lent him by a woman of high rank, (Lady Carbery ?), who, though young herself, had known him from a child. Thus scantily provided for, he walked off to North Wales, where he rambled for months, and finally made his way to London, in some hopes of raising money on the portion to which he would be entitled at the age of twenty-one.

What appeared in the London Magazine, in 1821, as "Confessions of an English Opium Eater," contains a narrative of his adventures in Wales and London — a story too full of interest in its details to be here condensed. Suffice it to say, that during the months he remained in London, he suffered such depths of want and starvation, that, in after years, his health was greatly injured. His attempts to put the future in pledge for the present, by means of Jew money-lenders, wholly failed, but, in the worst extreme of his sufferings, an opening was made, almost by accident, for reconciliation with his friends. He quitted London, and finally matriculated at Oxford, at Christmas, 1803, being then in his nineteenth year. But his guardian, compelled to yield on this point, refused to sign an order for more than £100 a year, the allowance made to him at school, — double that sum being considered the lowest amount on which an undergraduate could then live at the University, — and the almost inevitable result was that, some eighteen months later, he had to borrow money from the Jews, on very usurious terms, which subsequently plunged him in pecuniary difficulties.

De Quincey remained at Oxford from 1803 to 1808, with occasional visits to London during terms and in the long vacation. He made some acquaintances with literary men. In the summer of 1803, he had introduced himself by letter to Wordsworth, but did not personally know him until five years later. He met Lamb as early as 1804, but did not thoroughly appreciate him until 1808, when they formed a mutual friendship, which continued for many years, down to 1827, without doubt. At this period, too, he became intimate with Sir Humphrey Davy, Mr. Godwin, Lady Hamilton, Hannah More, Walking Stewart, Mr. Hazlitt, Mr. Abernethy, and others. He also met Dr. Parr, for whose great pedantry and rude manners he expressed undisguised contempt in later years.

To this period also belongs De Quincey's personal knowledge of Coleridge. In 1804 or 1805 (as he states), he learned that Coleridge had for some time applied his whole mind to metaphysics and psychology — which then happened to be De Quincey's own absorbing pursuit at the time. He did not succeed in meeting him until 1807, at Bridgewater, in Somersetshire, and was so much delighted with him that, understanding him to labor under some pecuniary embarrassment, he "contrived that a particular service should be tendered to Mr. Coleridge, a week after, through the hands of Mr. Cottle, of Bristol, which might have the effect of liberating his mind from anxiety for a year or two, and thus rendering his great powers disposable to their natural uses. That service was accepted by Coleridge. To save him any feelings of distress, all names were concealed," — but De Quincey learned from himself, fifteen years later, that Coleridge was cognizant, from the first, of the author of his munificence. De Quincey's own account, here quoted, is delicate and forbearing. The facts, as related in Mr. Cottle's Reminiscences, are so much to De Quincey's credit that they should not be omitted here. When De Quincey first met Cottle, he inquired into Coleridge's pecuniary affairs, and asked whether he would accept one or two hundred pounds. Coleridge was applied to, declared that pecuniary pressures of the moment were the only serious obstacles to the completion of several works, which, if completed, would make him easy, and that he would accept the money as an unconditional loan. On learning this, De Quincey immediately declared that he would *give* five hundred pounds, provided the source whence this bounty flowed was never named to Coleridge. At this time, De Quincey was twenty-two years old, and the intended gift was a *tenth* of his whole patrimony. On Mr. Cottle's earnest suggestion, the amount bestowed was reduced to £300. De Quincey never ascertained whether this service was of serious benefit to Coleridge; it has been ascertained by others that a large portion of it had been spent in procuring opium, to the use of which Coleridge was addicted all his life. The generosity of De Quincey is not lessened by the misuse of his princely gift.

Immediately after this transaction, in the fall of 1817, De Quincey proceeded to the lakes (accompanying Mrs. Coleridge and her three children) to see Wordsworth, then residing in a small cottage at Grasmere, between Ambleside and Keswick, and then, also, he first met Southey. So much pleased was he with the country and these new friends, that, in the following year, he took Wordsworth's cottage on a seven years' lease, and, indeed, had his domicil during the next twenty years amongst the lakes and mountains of Westmoreland. He made visits, southwards in England, and northward in Scotland; but nine months out of every twelve, between 1808 and 1829, he lived in Westmoreland.

Here he applied himself, very successfully, to the study of metaphysics and German. Here he extended his literary acquaintanceship, meeting Wilson at Wordsworth's, and Charles Lloyd also. In 1814, on a visit to the mother of the late Professor Wilson, he first went to Edinburgh, and among the earliest of his friends there may be named Sir William Hamilton, the present venerable Professor of Logic in the University. These visits to Scotland were frequently renewed, particularly after Wilson was made Professor of Moral Philosophy in 1820, and in 1832 he was induced to take his permanent residence there.

It was in Westmoreland also that De Quincey married. The exact date is not known, nor has he anywhere mentioned the lady's maiden name — but, in his Literary Reminiscences, at the date of November, 1807, apostrophizing his wife, he says, "Thou wert at present a child not nine years old, nor had I seen thy face, nor heard thy name. But within nine years (1816) from that same night, thou wert seated by my side; — and, thenceforwards, through a period of fourteen years (1830), how often did we two descend, hand locked in hand, and thinking of things to come, at a pace of hurricane." Of this marriage, which was a very happy union, several daughters were the issue.

It now becomes necessary to go back to the autumn of 1804, when De Quincey, then nineteen years old, took some tincture of opium, on the recommendation of a friend, to alleviate the pains of a severe attack of rheumatism in the head. The specific removed the pains, but also created such a pleasurable sort of intellectual excitement, that its use was adopted and continued for ten years. This habit of constant use was continued through the earlier years of De Quincey's residence at Grasmere. His health did not appear injuriously affected during the first eight years, 1804 to 1812; but in the course of 1813, there was a renewal of a severe irritation of the stomach, the result of his miserable starvation months in London. To mitigate the suffering thus caused, he increased the frequency and quantity of his opium-takings, until, at last, his doses amounted to 320 grains of opium, or 8000 drops per diem — an amount, large though it be, little more (Southey has stated) than half what Coleridge had accustomed himself to at the very same time. But, by 1816 (probably when he was about being married), De Quincey determined to break himself, if possible, of the baneful practice. He reduced his daily dose from 340 grains to 40, and the "Confessions" detail, with impressive power of description and expression, the pleasures and the pains of opium-taking. Thrice was the effort made to abandon the habit — twice it failed. At last, by a strong effort of the will, opium was wholly abandoned, leaving the body indeed weak, but the intellect if not stronger, at least more self-reliant and fructifying than before. In the "Confessions," he records, in beautiful and touching language, how greatly he was indebted to the tender and watchful affection of his wife. He says, after comparing himself to the dream-haunted Orestes, "My Eumenides, like his, were at my bed-feet, and stared in upon me through the curtains; but, watching by my pillow, or defrauding herself of sleep to bear me company through the heavy watches of the night, sat my Electra; for thou, beloved M., dear companion of my later years, thou wast my Electra! and neither in nobility of mind nor in long-suffering affection, wouldst permit that a Grecian sister should excel an English wife. For thou thoughtest not much to stoop to humble offices of kindness, and to servile ministrations of tenderest affection; to wipe away for years the unwholesome dews upon the forehead, or to refresh the lips when parched and baked with fever; nor even when thy own peaceful slumbers had by long sympathy become infected with the spectacle of my dread contest with phantoms and shadowy enemies, that oftentimes bade me 'sleep no more!' — not even then didst thou utter a complaint or any murmur, nor withdraw thy angelic smiles, nor shrink from thy service of love, more than Electra did of old. For she, too, though a Grecian woman, and the daughter of the King of men, yet wept sometimes, and hid her face in her robe."

In 1821, after he had been five years married, during which time three children were born to him, De Quincey was compelled, by pressing pecuniary embarrassments, to endeavor to extricate himself by literature. At that time he was thirty-six years old, in the fulness of mental strength, but with his bodily health much shaken by, and suffering from, the injurious effects of excessive indulgence in the use of opium. He proceeded to London, where he had many literary friends, and had no difficulty in obtaining an engagement as contributor to the London Magazine — a periodical of much worth and promise at the time, with an array of writers which included some of the most brilliant then in England. He has enumerated among them, Charles Lamb, Hazlitt, Allan Cunningham, Thomas Hood, Hamilton Reynolds, Carey (the translator of Dante), Crow, the public orator of Cambridge, John Clare (the Northamptonshire peasant poet), Charles Phillips, Talfourd, and John Taylor, one of the publishers of the Magazine, a political economist of some note, and author of the ablest work yet written to identify Sir Philip Francis with the authorship of Junius.

De Quincey's original intention was simply to supply translations from the best German writers, — Germany being a literary field in which, at that time, scarcely any English ploughshare had turned up a furrow. But it was known how his health had suffered from the use and abuse of opium, and the eloquent manner in which he spoke of the pleasures and pains caused by that nepenthe, caused the suggestion — the request — that he would relate his experiences. Accordingly, in the autumn of 1821, he wrote the greater part of the "Confessions of an English Opium-Eater." He has recorded, that "the narrative part was written with singular rapidity," while that portion relating to his dreams was much more slowly composed, from the pain of recollecting the sufferings by which he had been all but utterly prostrated. The first portion, which appeared in the London Magazine in 1821, was immediately and immensely popular. Its originality and its power struck a fresh key on the public mind, and when the work was presented, in a collected form, as a book, in 1822, its sale was unusually great. It has gone through numerous editions in England, and at once placed its author in the front rank of vivid and powerful writers. Not until 1845 did a continuation appear (in Blackwood's Magazine), under the title of "Suspiria de Profundis." More unequal, more desultory, less concentrated than the original "Confessions," it yet contains many powerful, and sometimes even brilliant passages. It is less unequal, indeed, than might have been anticipated from the circumstance of its emanating from the resumption of a work of great merit after the lapse of nearly quarter of a century.

The "Suspiria" appeared avowedly as a *sequel* to the "Confessions,"— but it does not complete the work according to De Quincey's own ideal. Two other portions were avowedly in his contemplation — one to be entitled "The Pariah World," and the other "The Kingdom of Darkness." As it is, therefore, confessedly incomplete (though not imperfect, for it is entirely *sui generis* and perfect as far as it goes), it may be looked upon as a literary *torso*, the beauty of the whole to be judged from the fragment which we possess.

The "Confessions," and, indeed, the whole of De Quincey's works, were written under no stronger external excitement than that supplied by the herb which cheers but does not inebriate. He has himself said, "I usually drink tea from eight o'clock at night to four in the morning." It was between those hours that he studied and wrote, while in London in 1821–23, and the habit has not been wholly relinquished at the present hour.

The success of the "Confessions" placed De Quincey at once in a high position as a writer, and his contributions to the periodical press were paid for at a large price. In 1824, when the German booksellers, in the absence of a new Waverley Novel, produced "Walladmor, by Sir Walter Scott," an early copy of the forgery was placed in De Quincey's hands, and by him rapidly reviewed for the London Magazine. The extracts which he gave awakened so much curiosity that the translation and English publication of the work was determined on. It appeared, on closer examination, so deficient in merit, that De Quincey had to re-write and re-cast the greater portion of it. In this guise was it published; and, written against time as it was, deserves to be considered, from its own claims, as well as the circumstances which produced it, one of the literary curiosities of the time.

In 1825, De Quincey contributed to Knight's Quarterly Magazine, the periodical in which some of Macaulay's earliest prose and poetry appeared. As early as October, 1825, De Quincey was recognized, by the wits of Blackwood's Magazine, by being introduced as an interlocutor at the "Noctes Ambrosianæ." On other occasions he was similarly honored, and was invariably mentioned with praise by Wilson, the presiding genius of Maga. He was easily induced to join the contributors, and his first avowed articles, called the "Gallery of the German Prose Classics," were commenced in Blackwood for November, 1826. The series opened with Lessing, and a subsequent paper was devoted to Kant. From that period De Quincey has occasionally been a large, though desultory contributor to Blackwood, and some of his best papers have appeared in that periodical.

In 1832, he appears to have determined to make Edinburgh his future residence. At that time, William Tait, an enterprising publisher, of ultra-liberal opinions, established Tait's Edinburgh Magazine, as a counterpoise to Blackwood's, which was the child and champion of Scottish Toryism. At that time, the great political question of the day was Parliamentary Reform, — declared by one party to be indispensable for the preservation of the British Empire, denounced by another party as revolutionary in the extreme. Tait was on the popular side. De Quincey's avowed politics were on the other. But publisher and author agreed in thinking that literature proper was of no particular politics nor party, and, liberal terms being offered, De Quincey became a contributor to Tait, and the "Literary Reminiscences" which now constitute two volumes in the American collection of his writings, were first given to the world through that periodical. He has also contributed largely to the Encyclopedia Britannica, the North British Review, Hogg's Weekly Instructor, and other less known periodicals. In 1837, he resumed his connection with Blackwood, (producing that remarkable narrative, nearly all imaginary, called "Revolt of the Tartars; or the Flight of the Kalmuck Khan and his people from the Russian Territories to the Frontiers of China,") and, for some years enriched that periodical with a series of papers upon a variety of subjects, which certainly show him fully entitled to the title of myriad-minded man. Even yet, though old age has overtaken him, in addition to constant ill health, "the old man eloquent" has not relinquished the pen.

De Quincey has written upon a wider and more diversified range of subjects than any other author of his time. Theology, metaphysics, political economy, criticism, history, philosophy, biography, astronomy, fiction, classical and German literature, have by turns engaged his attention, as well as essays on literature and men of letters, and narratives of singular force and merit. Scattered as his writings are over a variety of periodicals, during a period of nearly five-and-thirty years, it is probable that no collection of them would have been undertaken in England, (partly from the difficulty of ascertaining the identity of all, and partly because of the claims on their copyrights by different publishers,) if Messrs. Ticknor & Fields, of Boston, had not ventured on the somewhat hazardous task — the result being not only pecuniary success, in which they have voluntarily permitted the author to participate, but the thus making De Quincey's writings known to the new generation of readers who have sprung up since he first appeared in print. This success, also, echoing back to his cottage at Lasswade, near Edinburgh, (a picturesque situation, on which Scott happily passed the first few years of his manhood, where he vibrated between obscurity and fame,) has induced him to collect and revise for republication in England, such of his writings as he desired deliberately to avow. And thus, from this country, the very existence of whose literature was challenged by an Edinburgh reviewer, within the memory of men not yet aged, has sped across the wide Atlantic a hearty and cheering recognition, in his later years, of the genius of Thomas De Quincey.

The "Confessions of an English Opium-Eater," unquestionably show that the writer is gifted in no ordinary degree. Had he rested upon this, De Quincey would have attained a reputation scarcely inferior to that of any prose writer in the language. But "dura necessitas, et res angustæ domi," compelled him to belong to the class who do not live to write, but write to live. Hence, his powers have been frittered away, in a manner, in magazine writing, — the most exhausting, perhaps, of all sorts of composition. Hence, with the additional drawback of ill health and depressed spirits, (which have often obstructed him in writing,) he has scarcely given any decided and substantive proof of the great powers which he undoubtedly possesses. He has not done justice to himself.

It would have been well had his other writings possessed the earnestness and intensity of his "Confessions." But — one of the results, almost inevitable, perhaps, of his writing for periodicals — he has fallen into the habit, not only of overlaying his thoughts with words, but of obstructing the free course of their expression by digressions, parentheses, and extraneous and desultory matter, bearing little direct relation to his subject. His reigning fault is want of concentration. He sometimes heaps words upon words, as if to show the richness of his vocabulary. No one who has read his "Confessions" can think him deficient in imagination — some of his word-pictures cannot be surpassed — but he rarely has indulged in this great power. His learning, unquestionably great, has too often led him into pedantry. On a few occasions (such as "Murder Considered as one of the Fine Arts," in which the title is the most suggestive part of the paper,) he has attempted to be humorous. That he has scarcely succeeded may be attributed to his greater appreciation of the higher faculty of *wit*, which has disqualified him from the expression of what is merely ludicrous. A writer in the *Westminster Review*, of acknowledged critical acumen, has thus summed up his conclusions: — "With a genius so original — with such stores of learning — such depth of insight, — and such subtlety of thought, — Mr. De Quincey has given us no one really great work. He has written on almost every subject, but has exhausted none. He has thrown out hints and suggestions of the utmost value, but has left it to others to follow them laboriously up. He has acquired a style of the rarest brilliancy and richness, but he is constantly diminishing his force — now by his capricious use of words, and now by the weary length of his digressions." But, whatever the defects of his *manner*, De Quincey's *matter* is good. He writes, whatever subject he takes up, from the fulness of his knowledge, and, considering the quantity he has carelessly flung off, and the circumstances under which he has produced it, Thomas De Quincey may fairly be placed among the great spirits of his time.

Even now, having passed the allotted threescore and ten years of human life, with his mind's natural force not abated, he fondly indulges in the dream of yet producing some separate work which the world will not willingly let die. That he can do so, no one need doubt. In his later years, — happily passed at

Lasswade, in the society of his children and within reach of frequent companionship with gifted friends, themselves most eminent, who admire the brilliant course of the author, and love the harmless and pure life of the man, — his mind may flourish

> "Like the Aloe flower,
> Which blooms and blossoms at fourscore."

"Klosterheim, or The Masque," written in the full maturity of Thomas De Quincey's mind, — at the age of forty-six, and only ten years after his first essay as author of "Confessions of an English Opium-Eater," — eminently deserves the designation of a Curiosity of Literature; and it is surprising that it was not particularly referred to, as such, in the last edition of the elder D'Israeli's work. It will be admitted that, even in his most discursive and expanded compositions, De Quincey gave evidence that he possessed rich fancy and high imagination, in conjunction with extensive erudition. It might have been expected, also, that when adventuring on a new path, as a writer of fiction, he would have taken his stand upon English ground and drawn from the varieties of English character and incident. But his great pride has been that he was one of the first to throw open the wealth of German literature — that El Dorado of the mind — to the notice of his countrymen, and his solitary romance has its scene, characters, and action, upon German soil. "Klosterheim" is as essentially a German story, as if it had been translated. From first to last, without pause, break, or digression, the plot is made conducive to a certain *dénoûement*, which the skill of the artist-author has contrived, with great adroitness, so as not to be suspected until the very termination of the story. The leading elements and characteristics of fiction — wild adventure, guilt-born terror, enduring love, and secret mystery — pervade the whole composition, which reads like a true narrative of actual events, so progressive are the incidents, so complete the *vrai-semblance*. In some scenes, the limits of the supernatural are reached, and the effect is startling. Into his service he has impressed hatred and love, revenge and remorse, fear and courage, mystery and terror; and, in the closing scenes, has freely made use of that response which keeps the reader breathless with expectation. — In the employment of mystery and terror, he awakens recollections of the wonderful art with which Mrs. Radcliffe extorted science from the same mighty agents. Like her, too, — and she is named head of the novelists who used such science — though he appears, at times, to pass into the supernatural, he never wholly abandons the actual. If he involves the characters in a cloud of mystery, he does not fail to dissipate it, at the proper crisis, with the ingenuity of a master of the art.

"Klosterheim," as a literary composition, is written in De Quincey's best style. Its language is full of concentration, and the story is never once impeded by the digressions and the waste of words, which, his warmest admirers admit, constitute the defective points in his subsequent writings. Another striking feature in "Klosterheim" is its truly dramatic character, — a feature so observable, indeed, that the story was simultaneously dramatized for two of the London theatres, and performed, during the greater part of the season, with great success. The melodramatic character of the story rendered it so readily applicable, that, with the exception of introducing a slight underplot, no material alteration was made by the playwrights.

The collected works of De Quincey would be as incomplete without "Klosterheim," as those of Byron without "English Bards," of Moore without the "Epicurean," of Coleridge without the fragment of "Christabel," or of Scott without the "Talisman." Composed in the prime of his life, when his mental and bodily health were better than they had been for years, the romance of Klosterheim may be taken as one of those labors of love, conceived in a happy moment and executed in a happy mood. It will be for the public to determine why an author who had so ably acquitted himself in this new field of thought, should have not cultivated it more industriously. At all events, "Klosterheim" stands among De Quincey's numerous writings, as the only complete and extensive effort of his "imagination all compact."

KLOSTERHEIM.

CHAPTER I.

The winter of 1633 had set in with unusual severity throughout Suabia and Bavaria, though as yet scarcely advanced beyond the first week of November. It was, in fact, at the point when our tale commences, the 8th of that month, or, in our modern computation, the 18th; long after which date it had been customary of late years, under any ordinary state of the weather, to extend the course of military operations, and without much decline of vigor. Latterly, indeed, it had become apparent that entire winter campaigns, without either formal suspensions of hostilities, or even partial relaxations, had entered professedly as a point of policy into the system of warfare which now swept over Germany in full career, threatening soon to convert its vast central provinces — so recently blooming Edens of peace and expanding prosperity — into a howling wilderness; and which had already converted immense tracts into one universal aceldama, or human shambles, reviving to the recollection at every step the extent of past happiness in the endless memorials of its destruction. This innovation upon the old practice of war had been introduced by the Swedish armies, whose northern habits and training had fortunately prepared them to receive a German winter as a very beneficial exchange; whilst upon the less hardy soldiers from Italy, Spain, and the Southern France, to whom the harsh transition from their own sunny skies had made the very same climate a severe trial of constitution, this change of policy pressed with a hardship that sometimes * crippled their exertions.

It was a change, however, not so long settled as to resist the extraordinary circumstances of the weather. So fierce had been the cold for the last fortnight, and so premature, that a pretty confident anticipation had arisen, in all quarters throughout the poor exhausted land, of a general armistice. And as this, once established, would offer a ready opening to some measure of permanent pacification, it could not be surprising that the natural hopefulness of the human heart, long oppressed by gloomy prospects, should open with

* Of which there is more than one remarkable instance, to the great dishonor of the French arms, in the records of *her* share in the Thirty Years' War.

unusual readiness to the first colorable dawn of happier times. In fact, the reaction in the public spirits was sudden and universal. It happened also that the particular occasion of this change of prospect brought with it a separate pleasure on its own account. Winter, which, by its peculiar severity, had created the apparent necessity for an armistice, brought many household pleasures in its train — associated immemorially with that season in all northern climates. The cold which had casually opened a path to more distant hopes, was also for the present moment a screen between themselves and the enemy's sword. And thus it happened that the same season, which held out a not improbable picture of final restoration, however remote, to public happiness, promised them a certain foretaste of this blessing in the immediate security of their homes.

But in the ancient city of Klosterheim it might have been imagined that nobody participated in these feelings. A stir and agitation amongst the citizens had been conspicuous for some days; and on the morning of the 8th, spite of the intense cold, persons of every rank were seen crowding from an early hour to the city walls, and returning homewards at intervals, with anxious and dissatisfied looks. Groups of both sexes were collected at every corner of the wider streets, keenly debating, or angrily protesting; at one time denouncing vengeance to some great enemy; at another, passionately lamenting some past or half-forgotten calamity, recalled to their thoughts whilst anticipating a similar catastrophe for the present day.

Above all, the great square, upon which the ancient castellated palace or *schloss* opened by one of its fronts, as well as a principal convent of the city, was the resort of many turbulent spirits. Most of these were young men, and amongst them many students of the university: for the war, which had thinned or totally dispersed some of the greatest universities in Germany, under the particular circumstances of its situation had greatly increased that of Klosterheim. Judging by the tone which prevailed, and the random expressions which fell upon the ear at intervals, a stranger might conjecture that it was no empty lamentation over impending evils which occupied this crowd, but some serious preparation for meeting or redressing them. An officer of some distinction had been for some time observing them from the antique portals of the palace. It was probable, however, that little more than their gestures had reached him; for at length he moved nearer, and gradually insinuated himself into the thickest part of the mob, with the air of one who took no further concern in their proceedings, than that of simple curiosity. But his martial air and his dress allowed him no means of covering his purpose. With more warning and leisure to arrange his precautions, he might have passed as an indifferent spectator; as it was, his jewel-hilted sabre, the massy gold chain, depending in front from a costly button and loop which secured it half way down his back, and his broad crimson scarf, embroidered in a style of peculiar splendor, announced him as a favored officer of the Landgrave, whose ambitious pretensions, and tyrannical mode of supporting them, were just now the objects of general abhorrence in Klosterheim. His own appearance did not belie the service which he had adopted. He was a man of stout person, somewhat elegantly formed, in age about three or four-and-thirty, though perhaps a year or two of his apparent age might be charged upon the bronzing effects of sun and wind. In bearing and carriage, he announced to every eye the mixed carelessness and self-possession of a military training ; and as his features were regular, and remarkably intelligent, he would have been pronounced, on the whole, a man of winning exterior, were it not for the repulsive effect of his eye, in which there was a sinister expression of treachery, and at times a ferocious one of cruelty.

Placed upon their guard by his costume, and the severity of his countenance, those of the lower rank were silent as he moved along, or lowered their voices into whispers and inaudible murmurs. Amongst the students, however, whenever they happened to muster strongly, were many fiery young men, who disdained to temper the expression of their feelings, or to moderate their tone. A large group of these at one corner of the square drew attention upon themselves, as well by the conspicuous station which they occupied upon the steps of a church portico, as by the loudness of their voices. Towards them the officer directed his steps; and probably no lover of *scenes* would have had very long to wait for some explosion between parties, both equally ready to take offence, and careless of giving it; but at that moment, from an opposite angle of the square, was seen approaching a young man in plain clothes, who drew off the universal regard of the mob upon himself, and by the uproar of welcome which saluted him, occasioned all other sounds to be stifled. "Long life to our noble leader!" — "Welcome to the good Max!" resounded through the square. "Hail to our noble brother!" was the acclamation of the students. And everybody hastened forward to meet him with an impetuosity, which, for the moment, drew off all attention from the officer; he was left standing by himself on the steps of the church, looking down upon this scene of joyous welcome — the sole spectator who neither fully understood its meaning, nor shared in its feelings.

The stranger, who wore in part the antique costume of the university of Klosterheim, except where he still retained underneath a travelling dress, stained with recent marks of the roads and the weather, advanced amongst his friends with an air at once frank, kind, and dignified. He replied to their greetings in the language of cheerfulness; but his features expressed anxiety, and his manner was hurried. Whether he had not observed the officer overlooking them, or thought that the importance of the communications which he had to make transcended all common restraints of caution, there was little time to judge; so it was, at any rate, that without lowering his voice, he entered abruptly upon his business.

"Friends! I have seen the accursed Holkerstein; I have penetrated within his fortress. With my own eyes I have viewed and numbered his vile assassins. They are in strength triple the utmost amount of our friends. Without help from us, our kinsmen are lost. Scarce one of us but will lose a dear friend before three nights are over, should Klosterheim not resolutely do her duty."

"She shall, she shall!" exclaimed a multitude of voices.

"Then, friends, it must be speedily; never was there more call for sudden resolution. Perhaps before to-morrow's sun shall set, the sword of this detested robber will be at their throats. For he has some intelligence (whence I know not, nor how much) of their approach. Neither think that Holkerstein is a man acquainted with any touch of mercy or relenting. Where no ransom is to be had, he is in those circumstances, that he will and must deliver himself from the burden of prisoners by a general massacre. Infants even will not be spared."

Many women had by this time flocked to the outer ring of the listening audience. And perhaps for *their* ears in particular it was that the young stranger urged these last circumstances; adding,

"Will you look down tamely from your city walls upon such another massacre of the innocents as we have once before witnessed?"

"Cursed be Holkerstein!" said a multitude of voices.

"And cursed be those that openly or secretly support him!" added one of the students, looking earnestly at the officer.

"Amen!" said the officer, in a solemn tone, and looking round him with the aspect of one who will not suppose himself to have been included in the suspicion.

"And, friends, remember this," pursued the popular favorite; "whilst you are discharging the first duties of Christians and brave men to those who are now throwing themselves upon the hospitality of your city, you will also be acquitting yourselves of a great debt to the Emperor."

"Softly, young gentleman, softly," interrupted the officer; "his Serene Highness, my liege lord and yours, governs here, and the Emperor has no part in our allegiance. For debts, what the city owes to the

Emperor, she will pay. But men and horses I take it — "

"Are precisely the coin which the time demands; these will best please the Emperor, and, perhaps, will suit the circumstances of the city. But, leaving the Emperor's rights as a question for lawyers, — you, sir, are a soldier, — I question not, a brave one, — will you advise his Highness the Landgrave to look down from the castle windows upon a vile marauder, stripping or murdering the innocent people who are throwing themselves upon the hospitality of this ancient city?"

"Ay, sir, that will I, be you well assured — the Landgrave is my sovereign — "

"Since when? Since Thursday week, I think; for so long it is since your *tertia** first entered Klosterheim. But in that as you will, and if it be a point of honor with you gentlemen Walloons, to look on whilst women and children are butchered. For such a purpose no man is *my* sovereign; and as to the Landgrave in particular — "

"Nor ours, nor ours," shouted a tumult of voices, which drowned the young student's words about the Landgrave, though apparently part of them reached the officer. He looked round in quest of some military comrades who might support him in the *voye du*

* An old Walloon designation for a battalion.

fait, to which, at this point, his passion prompted him. But, seeing none, he exclaimed, "Citizens, press not this matter too far — and you, young man, especially forbear — you tread upon the brink of treason!"

A shout of derision threw back his words.

"Of treason, I say," he repeated furiously; "and such wild behavior it is, (and I say it with pain,) that perhaps even now is driving his Highness to place your city under martial law."

"Martial law! did you hear that?" ran along from mouth to mouth.

"Martial law, gentlemen, I say; how will you relish the little articles of that code? The Provost Martial makes short leave-takings. Two fathom of rope, and any of these pleasant old balconies which I see around me, (pointing, as he spoke, to the antique galleries of wood which ran round the middle stories in the convent of St. Peter,) with a confessor, or none, as the Provost's breakfast may chance to allow, have cut short, to my knowledge, the freaks of many a better fellow than any I now see before me."

Saying this, he bowed with a mock solemnity all round to the crowd, which, by this time, had increased in number and violence. Those who were in the outermost circles, and beyond the distinct hearing of what he said, had been discussing with heat the alarming confirmation of their fears in respect to Holkerstein, or listening to the impassioned narrative of a woman, who had already seen one of her sons butchered by this ruffian's people under the walls of the city, and was now anticipating the same fate for her last surviving son and daughter, in case they should happen to be amongst the party now expected from Vienna. She had just recited the tragical circumstances of her son's death, and had worked powerfully upon the sympathizing passions of the crowd, when, suddenly, at a moment so unseasonable for the officer, some imperfect repetition of his words about the Provost Marshal and the rope, passed rapidly from mouth to mouth. It was said that he had threatened every man with instant death at the drum-head, who should but speculate on assisting his friends outside, under the heaviest extremities of danger or of outrage. The sarcastic bow, and the inflamed countenance of the officer, were seen by glimpses farther than his words extended. Kindling eyes and lifted arms of many amongst the mob, and chiefly of those on the outside who had heard his words the most imperfectly, proclaimed to such as knew Klosterheim and its temper at this moment the danger in which he stood. Maximilian, the young student, generously forgot his indignation in concern for his immediate safety. Seizing him by the hand he exclaimed, —

"Sir, but a moment ago you warned me that I stood on the brink of treason, — look to your own safety at present; for the eyes of some whom I see yonder are dangerous."

"Young gentleman," the other replied contemptuously, "I presume that you are a student; let me counsel you to go back to your books. There you will be in your element. For myself, I am familiar with faces as angry as these — and hands something more formidable. Believe me, I see nobody here," and he affected to speak with imperturbable coolness, but his voice became tremulous with passion, "whom I can even esteem worthy of a soldier's consideration."

"And yet, Colonel von Aremberg, there is at least one man here who has had the honor of commanding men as elevated as yourself." Saying which, he hastily drew from his bosom, where it hung suspended from his neck, a large flat tablet of remarkably beautiful onyx, on one side of which was sculptured a very striking face; but on the other, which he presented to the gaze of the Colonel, was a fine representation of an eagle grovelling in the dust, and beginning to expand its wings — with the single word *Resurgam* by way of motto.

Never was revulsion of feeling so rapidly expresssed on any man's countenance. The Colonel looked but once — he caught the image of the bird trailing its pinions in the dust — he heard the word *Resurgam* audibly pronounced — his color fled — his lips grew livid with passion — and, furiously unsheathing his sword, he sprung, with headlong forgetfulness of time and place, upon his calm antagonist. With the advantage of perfect self-possession, Maximilian found it easy to parry the tempestuous blows of the Colonel; and he would perhaps have found it easy to disarm him. But at this moment the crowd, who had been with great difficulty represssed by the more thoughtful amongst the students, burst through all restraints. In the violent outrage offered to their champion and leader, they saw naturally a full confirmation of the worst impressions they had received as to the Colonel's temper and intention. A number of them rushed forward to execute summary vengeance; and the foremost amongst these, a mechanic of Klosterheim distinguished for his Herculean strength, with one blow stretched Von Aremberg on the ground. A savage yell announced the dreadful fate which impended over the fallen officer. And spite of the generous exertions made for his protection by Maximilian and his brother students, it is probable that at that moment no human interposition could have availed to turn aside the awakened appetite for vengeance, and that he must have perished, but for the accident which at that particular instant of time occurred to draw off the attention of the mob.

A signal gun from a watch-tower, which always in those unhappy times announced the approach of strangers, had been fired about ten minutes before;

but, in the turbulent uproar of the crowd, it had passed unnoticed. Hence it was, that, without previous warning to the mob assembled at this point, a mounted courier now sprung into the square at full gallop on his road to the palace, and was suddenly pulled up by the dense masses of human beings.

"News, news!" exclaimed Maximilian; "tidings of our dear friends from Vienna!" This he said with the generous purpose of diverting the infuriated mob from the unfortunate Von Aremberg, though himself apprehending that the courier had arrived from another quarter. His plan succeeded; the mob rushed after the horseman, all but two or three of the most sanguinary, who, being now separated from all assistance, were easily drawn off from their prey. The opportunity was eagerly used to carry off the Colonel, stunned and bleeding, within the gates of a Franciscan convent. He was consigned to the medical care of the holy fathers; and Maximilian, with his companions, then hurried away to the chancery of the palace, whither the courier had proceeded with his despatches.

These were interesting in the highest degree. It had been doubted by many, and by others a pretended doubt had been raised to serve the Landgrave's purpose, whether the great cavalcade from Vienna would be likely to reach the entrance of the forest for a week or more. Certain news had now arrived, and was published before it could be stifled, that they and all their baggage, after a prosperous journey so far, would be assembled at that point on this very evening. The courier had left the advanced guard about noonday, with an escort of four hundred of the Black Yagers from the Imperial Guard, and two hundred of Papenheim's Dragoons at Waldenhausen, on the very brink of the forest. The main body and rear were expected to reach the same point in four or five hours ; and the whole party would then fortify their encampment as much as possible against the night attack which they had too much reason to apprehend.

This was news which, in bringing a respite of forty-eight hours, brought relief to some who had feared that even this very night might present them with the spectacle of their beloved friends engaged in a bloody struggle at the very gates of Klosterheim ; for it was the fixed resolution of the Landgrave to suffer no diminution of his own military strength, or of the means for recruiting it hereafter. Men, horses, arms, all alike were rigorously laid under embargo by the existing government of the city ; and such was the military power at its disposal, reckoning not merely the numerical strength in troops, but also the power of sweeping the main streets of the town, and several of the principal roads outside, that it was become a matter of serious doubt whether the unanimous insurrection of the populace had a chance for making head against the government. But others found not even a momentary comfort on this account. They considered that perhaps Waldenhausen might be the very ground selected for the murderous attack. There was here a solitary post-house, but no town or even village. The forest at this point was just thirty-four miles broad; and if the bloodiest butchery should be going on under cover of night, no rumor of it could be borne across the forest in time to alarm the many anxious friends who would this night be lying awake in Klosterheim.

A slight circumstance served to barb and point the public distress, which otherwise seemed previously to have reached its utmost height. The courier had brought a large budget of letters to private individuals throughout Klosterheim; many of these were written by children unacquainted with the dreadful catastrophe which threatened them. Most of them had been long separated, by the fury of the war, from their parents. They had assembled, from many different quarters, at Vienna, in order to join what might be called, in Oriental phrase, *the caravan.* Their parents had also, in many instances, from places equally dispersed, assembled at Klosterheim, — and, after great revolutions of fortune, they were now going once more to rejoin each other. Their letters expressed the feelings of hope and affectionate pleasure suitable to the occasion. They retraced the perils they had passed during the twenty-six days of their journey, — the great towns, heaths, and forests they had traversed since leaving the gates of Vienna; and expressed, in the innocent terms of childhood, the pleasure they felt in having come within two stages of the gates of Klosterheim. "In the forest," said they, "there will be no more dangers to pass; no soldiers; nothing worse than wild deer."

Letters written in these terms, contrasted with the mournful realities of the case, sharpened the anguish of fear and suspense throughout the whole city; and Maximilian with his friends, unable to bear the loud expression of the public feelings, separated themselves from the tumultuous crowds, and adjourning to the seclusion of their college rooms, determined to consult, whilst it was yet not too late, whether, in their hopeless situation for openly resisting the Landgrave without causing as much slaughter as they sought to prevent, it might not yet be possible for them to do something in the way of resistance to the bloody purposes of Holkerstein.

CHAPTER II.

The travelling party, for whom so much anxiety was felt in Klosterheim, had this evening reached Waldenhausen without loss or any violent alarm; and indeed, considering the length of their journey, and the distracted state of the empire, they had hitherto travelled in remarkable security. It was now nearly a month since they had taken their departure from Vienna, at which point considerable numbers had assembled from the adjacent country to take the benefit of their convoy. Some of these they had dropped at different turns in their route, but many more had joined them as they advanced; for in every considerable city they found large accumulations of strangers, driven in for momentary shelter from the storm of war as it spread over one district after another; and many of these were eager to try the chances of a change, or, upon more considerate grounds, preferred the protection of a place situated like Klosterheim, in a nook as yet unvisited by the scourge of military execution. Hence it happened, that from a party of seven hundred and fifty, with an escort of four hundred yagers, which was the amount of their numbers on passing through the gates of Vienna, they had gradually swelled into a train of sixteen hundred, including two companies of dragoons who had joined them by the Emperor's orders at one of the fortified posts.

It was felt, as a circumstance of noticeable singularity, by most of the party, that, after traversing a large part of Germany, without encountering any very imminent peril, they should be first summoned to unusual vigilance, and all the most jealous precautions of fear, at the very termination of their journey. In all parts of their route they had met with columns of troops pursuing their march, and now and then with roving bands of deserters, who were formidable to the unprotected traveller. Some they had overawed by their display of military strength; from others, in the Imperial service, they had received cheerful assistance; and any Swedish corps, which rumor had presented as formidable by their numbers, they had, with some exertion of forethought and contrivance, constantly evaded, either by a little detour, or by a temporary halt in some place of strength. But now it was universally known that they were probably waylaid by a desperate and remorseless freebooter, who, as he put his own trust exclusively in the sword, allowed nobody to hope for any other shape of deliverance.

Holkerstein, the military robber, was one of the

many monstrous growths which had arisen upon the ruins of social order in this long and unhappy war. Drawing to himself all the malecontents of his own neighborhood, and as many deserters from the regular armies in the centre of Germany as he could tempt to his service by the license of unlimited pillage, he had rapidly created a respectable force — had possessed himself of various castles in Wirtemberg, within fifty or sixty miles of Klosterheim — had attacked and defeated many parties of regular troops sent out to reduce him — and by great activity and local knowledge had raised himself to so much consideration, that the terror of his name had spread even to Vienna; and the escort of yagers had been granted by the Imperial government as much on his account as for any more general reason. A lady, who was in some way related to the Emperor's family, and, by those who were in the secret, was reputed to be the Emperor's natural daughter, accompanied the travelling party, with a suite of female attendants. To this lady, who was known by the name of the Countess Paulina, the rest of the company held themselves indebted for their escort; and hence, as much as for her rank, she was treated with ceremonious respect throughout the journey.

The Lady Paulina travelled with her suite in coaches, drawn by the most powerful artillery horses, that could be furnished at the various military posts.* On this day she had been in the rear; and having been delayed by an accident, she was waited for with some impatience by the rest of the party, the latest of whom had reached Waldenhausen early in the afternoon. It was sunset before her train of coaches arrived; and, as the danger from Holkerstein commenced about this point, they were immediately applied to the purpose of strengthening their encampment against a night attack, by chaining them, together with all the baggage carts, in a triple line, across the different avenues which seemed most exposed to a charge of cavalry. Many other preparations were made; the yagers and dragoons made arrangements for mounting with ease on the first alarm; strong outposts were established; sentinels posted all round the encampment, who were duly relieved every hour, in consideration of the extreme cold; and upon the whole, as many veteran officers were amongst them, the great body of the travellers were now able to apply themselves to the task of preparing their evening refreshments with some degree of comfort; for the elder part of the company saw that every precaution had been taken, and the younger were not aware of any extraordinary danger.

* Coaches were common in Germany at this time amongst people of rank: at the reinstatement of the Dukes of Mecklenburgh, by Gustavus Adolphus, though without much notice, more than fourscore of coaches were assembled.

Waldenhausen had formerly been a considerable village. At present there was no more than one house, surrounded, however, by such a large establishment of barns, stables, and other outhouses, that, at a little distance, it wore the appearance of a tolerable hamlet. Most of the outhouses, in their upper stories, were filled with hay or straw; and there the women and children prepared their couches for the night, as the warmest resorts in so severe a season. The house was furnished in the plainest style of a farmer's; but in other respects it was of a superior order, being roomy and extensive. The best apartment had been reserved for the Lady Paulina and her attendants; one for the officers of most distinction in the escort or amongst the travellers; the rest had been left to the use of the travellers indiscriminately.

In passing through the hall of entrance, Paulina had noticed a man of striking and *farouche* appearance, hair black and matted, eyes keen and wild, and beaming with malicious cunning, who surveyed her as she passed with a mixed looked of insolence and curiosity that involuntarily made her shrink. He had been half-reclining carelessly against the wall, when she first entered, but rose upright with a sudden motion as she passed him — not probably from any sentiment of respect, but under the first powerful impression of surprise on seeing a young woman of peculiarly splendid figure and impressive beauty, under circumstances so little according with what might be suposed her natural pretensions. The dignity of her deportment, and the numbers of her attendants, sufficiently proclaimed the luxurious accommodations which her habits might have taught her to expect; and she was now entering a dwelling which of late years had received few strangers of her sex, and probably none but those of the lowest rank.

"Know your distance, fellow!" exclaimed one of the waiting women angrily, noticing his rude gaze, and the effect upon her mistress.

"Good faith, madam, I would that the distance between us were more; it was no prayers of mine, I promise you, that brought upon me a troop of horses to Waldenhausen, enough in one twelve hours to eat me out a margrave's ransom. Light thanks I reckon on from yagers; and the payments of dragoons will pass current for as little in the forest, as a lady's frown in Waldenhausen."

"Churl!" said an officer of dragoons, "how know you that our payments are light? The Emperor takes nothing without payment; surely not from such as you. But *à propos* of ransoms, what now might be Holkerstein's ransom for a farmer's barns stuffed with a three years' crop?"

"How mean you by that, captain? The crop's my own, and never was in worse hands than my own. God send it no worse luck to-day!"

"Come, come, sir, you understand me better than that; nothing at Waldenhausen, I take it, is yours or any man's, unless by license from Holkerstein. And when I see so many goodly barns and garners, with their jolly charges of hay and corn, that would feed one of Holkerstein's garrisons through two sieges, I know what to think of him who has saved them scot-free. He that serves a robber must do it on a robber's terms. To such bargains, there goes but one word; and that is the robber's. But come, man, I am not thy judge. Only I would have my soldiers on their guard at one of Holkerstein's outposts. And thee, farmer, I would have to remember that an Emperor's grace may yet stand thee in stead, when a robber is past helping thee to a rope."

The soldiers laughed, but took their officer's hint to watch the motions of a man, whose immunity from spoil, in circumstances so tempting to a military robber's cupidity, certainly argued some collusion with Holkerstein.

The Lady Paulina had passed on during this dialogue into an inner room, hoping to have found the quiet and the warmth which were now become so needful to her repose. But the antique stove was too much out of repair to be used with benefit; the wood-work was decayed, and admitted currents of cold air; and, above all, from the slightness of the partitions, the noise and tumult in a house occupied by soldiers and travellers proved so incessant, that, after taking refreshments with her attendants, she resolved to adjourn for the night to her coach; which afforded much superior resources, both in warmth and in freedom from noise.

The carriage of the Countess was one of those which had been posted at an angle of the encampment, and on that side terminated the line of defences; for a deep mass of wood, which commenced where the carriages ceased, seemed to present a natural protection on that side against the approach of cavalry; in reality, from the quantity of tangled roots and the inequalities of the ground, it appeared difficult for a single horseman to advance even a few yards without falling. And upon this side it had been judged sufficient to post a single sentinel.

Assured by the many precautions adopted, and by the cheerful language of the officer on guard, who attended her to the carriage door, Paulina, with one attendant, took her seat in the coach, where she had the means of fencing herself sufficiently from the cold by the weighty robes of minever and ermine which her ample wardrobe afforded; and the large dimensions of the coach enabled her to turn it to the use of a sofa or couch.

Youth and health sleep well; and with all the means and appliances of the Lady Paulina, wearied besides as she had been with the fatigue of a day's march, performed over roads almost impassable from roughness, there was little reason to think that she would miss the benefit of her natural advantages. Yet sleep failed to come, or came only by fugitive snatches, which presented her with tumultuous dreams — sometimes of the Emperor's court in Vienna, sometimes of the vast succession of troubled scenes and fierce faces that had passed before her since she had quitted that city. At one moment she beheld the travelling equipages and far-stretching array of her own party, with their military escort filing off by torchlight under the gateway of ancient cities; at another, the ruined villages, with their dismantled cottages — doors and windows torn off, walls scorched with fire, and a few gaunt dogs, with a wolf-like ferocity in their bloodshot eyes, prowling about the ruins, — objects that had really so often afflicted her heart. Waking from those distressing spectacles, she would fall into a fitful dose, which presented her with remembrances still more alarming; bands of fierce deserters, that eyed her travelling party with a savage rapacity which did not confess any powerful sense of inferiority; and in the very fields which they had once cultivated, now silent and tranquil from utter desolation, the mouldering bodies of the unoffending peasants, left unhonored with the rites of sepulture, in many places from the mere extermination of the whole rural population of their neighborhood. To these succeeded a wild chaos of figures, in which the dress and tawny features of Bohemian gipsies conspicuously prevailed, just as she had seen them of late making war on all parties alike; and in the person of their leader, her fancy suddenly restored to her a vivid resemblance of their suspicious host at their present quarters, and of the malicious gaze with which he had disconcerted her.

A sudden movement of the carriage awakened her, and, by the light of a lamp suspended from a projecting bough of a tree, she beheld, on looking out, the sallow countenance of the very man whose image had so recently infested her dreams. The light being considerably nearer to him than to herself, she could see without being distinctly seen; and, having already heard the very strong presumptions against this man's honesty, which had been urged by the officer, and without reply from the suspected party, she now determined to watch him.

CHAPTER III.

The night was pitch dark, and Paulina felt a momentary terror creep over her as she looked into the massy blackness of the dark alleys which ran up into the woods, forced into deeper shade under the glare of the lamps from the encampment. She now reflected with some alarm that the forest commenced at this point, stretching away (as she had been told) in some directions upwards of fifty miles; and that, if the post occupied by their encampment should be inaccessible on this side to cavalry, it might, however, happen that persons with the worst designs could easily penetrate on foot from the concealments of the forest, in which case she herself, and the splendid booty of her carriage, might be the first and easiest prey. Even at this moment, the very worst of those atrocious wretches whom the times had produced, might be lurking in concealment, with their eyes fastened upon the weak or exposed parts of the encampment, and waiting until midnight should have buried the majority of their wearied party into the profoundest repose, in order then to make a combined and murderous attack.

Under the advantages of sudden surprise and darkness, together with the knowledge which they would not fail to possess of every road and by-path in the woods, it could scarcely be doubted that they might strike a very effectual blow at the Vienna caravan, which had else so nearly completed their journey without loss or memorable privations; — and the knowledge which Holkerstein possessed of the short limits within which his opportunities were now circumscribed, would doubtless prompt him to some bold and energetic effort.

Thoughts unwelcome as these, Paulina found leisure to pursue, for the ruffian landlord had disappeared almost at the same moment when she first caught a glimpse of him. In the deep silence which succeeded, she could not wean herself from the painful fascination of imagining the very worst possibilities to which their present situation was liable. She imaged to herself the horrors of a *camisade*, as she had often heard it described; she saw, in apprehension, the savage band of confederate butchers, issuing from the profound solitudes of the forest, in white shirts drawn over their armor; she seemed to read the murderous features, lighted up by the gleam of lamps — the stealthy step, and the sudden gleam of sabres; then the yell of assault, the scream of agony, the camp floating with blood; the fury, the vengeance, the pursuit; — all these circumstances of scenes at that time too familiar to Germany, passed rapidly before her mind.

But after some time, as the tranquillity continued, her nervous irritation gave way to less agitating but profound sensibilities. Whither was her lover withdrawn from her knowledge? and why? and for how long a time? What an age it seemed since she had last seen him at Vienna! That the service upon which he was employed would prove honorable, she felt assured. But was it dangerous? Alas! in Germany there was none otherwise. Would it soon restore him to her society? And why had he been of late so unaccountably silent? Or again, *had* he been silent? Perhaps his letters had been intercepted, — nothing, in fact, was more common at that time. The rarity was, if by any accident a letter reached its destination. From one of the worst solicitudes incident to such a situation, Paulina was, however, delivered by her own nobility of mind, which raised her above the meanness of jealousy. Whatsoever might have happened, or into whatever situations her lover might have been thrown, she felt no fear that the fidelity of his attachment could have wandered or faltered for a moment; — that worst of pangs the Lady Paulina was raised above, equally by her just confidence in herself and in her lover. But yet, though faithful to her, might he not be ill? Might he not be languishing in some one of the many distresses incident to war? Might he not even have perished?

That fear threw her back upon the calamities and horrors of war; and insensibly her thoughts wandered round to the point from which they had started, of her own immediate situation. Again she searched with penetrating eyes the black avenues of the woods, as they lay forced almost into strong relief and palpable substance by the glare of the lamps. Again she fancied to herself the murderous hearts and glaring eyes which even now might be shrouded by the silent masses of forest which stretched before her, — when suddenly a single light shot its rays from what appeared to be a considerable distance in one of the avenues. Paulina's heart beat fast at this alarming spectacle. Immediately after, the light was shaded, or in some way disappeared. But this gave the more reason for terror. It was now clear that human beings were moving in the woods. No public road lay in that direction; nor in so unpopulous a region, could it be imagined that travellers were likely at that time to be abroad. From their own encampment, nobody could have any motive for straying to a distance on so severe a night, and at a time when he would reasonably draw upon himself the danger of being shot by the night guard.

This last consideration reminded Paulina suddenly, as of a very singular circumstance, that the appearance of the light had been followed by no challenge from the sentinel. And then first she remembered that for some time she had ceased to hear the sentinel's step, or the rattle of his bandoleers. Hastily looking along the path, she discovered too certainly, that the single sentinel posted on that side of their encampment was absent from his station. It might have been supposed that he had fallen asleep from the severity of the cold; but in that case the lantern which he carried attached to his breast would have continued to burn; whereas all traces of light had vanished from the path which he perambulated. The error was now apparent to Paulina, both in having appointed no more than one sentinel to this quarter, and also in the selection of his beat. There had been frequent instances throughout this war in which by means of a net, such as that carried by the Roman *retiarius* in the contests of the gladiators, and dexterously applied by two persons from behind, a sentinel had been suddenly muffled, gagged, and carried off, without much difficulty. For such a purpose it was clear that the present sentinel's range, lying by the margin of a wood from which his minutest movements could be watched at leisure by those who lay in utter darkness themselves, afforded every possible facility. Paulina scarcely doubted that he had been indeed carried off, in some such way, and not impossibly almost whilst she was looking on.

She would now have called aloud, and have alarmed the camp, — but at the very moment when she let down the glass, the savage landlord reappeared, and, menacing her with a pistol, awed her into silence. He bore upon his head a moderate-sized trunk, or portmanteau which appeared, by the imperfect light, to be that in which some despatches had been lodged from the Imperial government to different persons in Klosterheim. This had been cut from one of the carriages in her suite; and her anxiety was great on recollecting that, from some words of the Emperor's, she had reason to believe one at least of the letters which it conveyed to be in some important degree connected with the interests of her lover. Satisfied, however, that he would not find it possible to abscond with so burdensome an article in any direction that could save him from instant pursuit and arrest, she continued to watch for the moment when she might safely raise the alarm. But great was her consternation when she saw a dark figure steal from a thicket, receive the trunk from the other, and instantly retreat into the deepest recesses of the forest.

Her fears now gave way to the imminence of so important a loss; and she endeavored hastily to open the window of the opposite door. But this had been so effectually barricaded against the cold, that she failed in her purpose, and immediately turning back to the other side she called loudly — "Guard! guard!" The press of carriages, however, at this point, so far deadened her voice, that it was some time before the alarm reached the other side of the encampment distinctly enough to direct their motions to her summons. Half a dozen yagers and an officer at length presented themselves; but the landlord had disappeared, she knew not in what direction. Upon explaining the circumstances of the robbery, however, the officer caused his men to light a number of torches and advance into the wood. But the ground was so impracticable in most places from tangled roots and gnarled stumps of trees, that it was with difficulty they could keep their footing. They were also embarrassed by the crossing shadows from the innumerable boughs above them; and a situation of greater perplexity for effective pursuit it was scarcely possible to imagine. Everywhere they saw alleys, arched high overhead, and resembling the aisles of a cathedral, as much in form as in the perfect darkness which reigned in both at this solemn hour of midnight, stretching away apparently without end, but more and more obscure, until impenetrable blackness terminated the long vista. Now and then a dusky figure was seen to cross at some distance; but these were probably deer; and when loudly challenged by the yagers, no sound replied but the vast echoes of the forest. Between these interminable alleys, which radiated as from a centre at this point, there were generally thickets interposed. Sometimes the wood was more open, and clear of all undergrowth — shrubs, thorns, or brambles — for a considerable distance, so that a single file of horsemen might have penetrated for perhaps half a mile; but belts of thicket continually checked their progress, and obliged them to seek their way back to some one of the long vistas which traversed the woods between the frontiers of Suabia and Bavaria.

In this perplexity of paths, the officer halted his party to consider of his further course. At this moment one of the yagers protested that he had seen a man's hat and face rise above a thicket of bushes, apparently not more than one hundred and fifty yards from their own position. Upon that, the party were ordered to advance a little, and to throw in a volley as nearly as could be judged, into the very spot pointed out by the soldier. It seemed that he had not been mistaken; for a loud laugh of derision rose immediately a little to the left of the bushes. The laughter swelled upon the silence of the night, and in the next moment was taken up by another on the right, which again was echoed by a third on the rear. Peal after peal of tumultuous and scornful laughter resounded from the remoter solitudes of the forest; and the officer stood aghast to hear this proclamation of defiance from a multitude of enemies, where he had anticipated no more than the very party engaged in the robbery.

To advance in pursuit seemed now both useless and dangerous. The laughter had probably been designed expressly to distract his choice of road at a time when the darkness and intricacies of the ground had already made it sufficiently indeterminate. In which direction, out of so many whence he had heard the sounds, a pursuit could be instituted with any chance of being effectual, seemed now as hopeless a subject of deliberation as it was possible to imagine. Still, as he had been made aware of the great importance attached to the trunk, which might, very probably, contain despatches interesting to the welfare of Klosterheim, and the whole surrounding territory, he felt grieved to retire without some further attempt for its recovery. And he stood for a few moments irresolutely debating with himself, or listening to the opinions of his men.

His irresolution was very abruptly terminated. All at once, upon the main road from Klosterheim, at an angle about half a mile a-head, where it first wheeled into sight from Waldenhausen, a heavy, thundering trot was heard ringing from the frozen road, as of a regular body of cavalry advancing rapidly upon their encampment. There was no time to be lost; the officer instantly withdrew his yagers from the wood, posted a strong guard at the wood side, sounded the alarm throughout the camp, agreeably to the system of signals previously concerted, mounted about thirty men, whose horses and themselves were kept in perfect equipment during each of the night watches, and then advancing to the head of the barriers, prepared to receive the party of strangers in whatever character they should happen to present themselves.

All this had been done with so much promptitude

and decision, that on reaching the barriers, the officer found the strangers not yet come up. In fact, they had halted at a strong outpost about a quarter of a mile in advance of Waldenhausen; and though one or two patrollers came dropping in from by-roads on the forest heath, who reported them as enemies, from the indistinct view they had caught of their equipments, it had already become doubtful from their movements whether they would really prove so.

Two of their party were now descried upon the road, and nearly close up with the gates of Waldenhausen; they were accompanied by several of the guard from the outpost, and, immediately on being hailed, they exclaimed, "Friends, and from Klosterheim!"

He who spoke was a young cavalier, magnificent alike in his person, dress, and style of his appointments. He was superbly mounted, wore the decorations of a major-general in the Imperial service, and scarcely needed the explanations which he gave, to exonerate himself from the suspicion of being a leader of robbers, under Holkerstein. Fortunately enough, also, at a period when officers of the most distinguished merit were too often unfaithful to their engagements, or passed with so much levity from service to service, as to justify an indiscriminate jealousy of all who were not in the public eye, it happened that the officer of the watch, formerly, when mounting guard at the Imperial palace, had been familiar with the personal appearance of the cavalier, and could speak of his own knowledge to the favor which he had enjoyed at the Emperor's court. After short explanations, therefore, he was admitted, and thankfully welcomed in the camp; and the officer of the guard departed to receive with honor the generous volunteers at the outpost.

Meantime, the alarm, which was general throughout the camp, had assembled all the women to one quarter, where a circle of carriages had been formed for their protection. In their centre, distinguished by her height and beauty, stood the Lady Paulina, dispensing assistance from her wardrobe to any who were suffering from cold under this sudden summons to night air, and animating others, who were more than usually depressed, by the aids of consolation and of cheerful prospects. She had just turned her face away from the passage by which this little sanctuary communicated with the rest of the camp, and was in the act of giving directions to one of her attendants, when suddenly a well-known voice fell upon her ear. It was the voice of the stranger cavalier, whose natural gallantry had prompted him immediately to relieve the alarm which, unavoidably, he had himself created; in a few words, he was explaining to the assembled females of the camp, in what character, and with how many companions he had come. But a shriek from

Paulina interrupted him. Involuntarily she held out her open arms, and involuntarily she exclaimed, "Dearest Maximilian!" On his part, the young cavalier, for a moment or two at first, was almost deprived of speech, by astonishment and excess of pleasure. Bounding forward, hardly conscious of those who surrounded them, with a rapture of faithful love, he caught the noble young beauty into his arms, a movement to which, in the frank innocence of her heart, she made no resistance; folded her to his bosom, and impressed a fervent kiss upon her lips, whilst the only words that came to his own were, "Beloved Paulina! oh, most beloved lady! what chance has brought you hither?"

CHAPTER IV.

In those days of tragical confusion and of sudden catastrophe, alike for better or for worse, when the rendings asunder of domestic charities were often without an hour's warning, when re-unions were as dramatic and as unexpected as any which are exhibited on the stage, and too often separations were eternal, — the circumstances of the times concurred with the spirit of manners to sanction a tone of frank expression to the stronger passions, which the reserve of modern habits would not entirely license. And hence, not less than from the noble ingenuousness of their natures, the martial young cavalier and the superb young beauty of the Imperial house, on recovering themselves from their first transports, found no motives to any feeling of false shame, either in their own consciousness, or in the reproving looks of any who stood around them. On the contrary, as the grown-up spectators were almost exclusively female,, to whom the evidences of faithful love are never other than a serious subject, or naturally associated with the ludicrous; many of them expressed their sympathy with the scene before them by tears, and all of them in some way or other. Even in this age of more fastidious manners, it is probable that the tender interchanges of affection between a young couple rejoining each other after deep calamities, and standing on the brink of fresh, perhaps endless separations, would meet with something of the same indulgence from the least interested witnesses.

Hence the news was diffused through the camp with general satisfaction, that a noble and accomplished cavalier, the favored lover of their beloved young mistress, had joined them from Klosterheim with a chosen band of volunteers, upon whose fidelity in action they might entirely depend. Some vague account floated about, at the same time, of the marauding attack upon the Lady Paulina's carriage. But naturally enough, from the confusion and hurry incident to a nocturnal disturbance, the circumstances were mixed up with the arrival of Maximilian, in the way which ascribed to him the merit of having repelled an attack, which might else have proved fatal to the lady of his heart. And this romantic interposition of Providence on a young lady's behalf, through the agency of her lover, unexpected on her part, and unconscious on his, proved so equally gratifying to the passion for the marvellous and the interest in youthful love, that no other or truer version of the case could ever obtain a popular acceptance in the camp, or afterwards in Klosterheim. And had it been the expiess purpose of

Maximilian to found a belief, for his own future benefit, of a providential sanction vouchsafed to his connection with the Lady Paulina, he could not, by the best arranged contrivances, have more fully attained that end.

It was yet short of midnight by more than an hour; and therefore, on the suggestion of Maximilian, who reported the roads across the forest perfectly quiet, and alleged some arguments for quieting the general apprehension for this night, the travellers and troops retired to rest, as the best means of preparing them to face the trials of the two next days. It was judged requisite, however, to strengthen the night-guard very considerably, and to relieve it at least every two hours. That the poor sentinel, on the forest side of the encampment, had been in some mysterious way trepanned upon his post, was now too clearly ascertained, for he was missing; and the character of the man, no less than the absence of all intelligible temptation to such an act, forbade the suspicion of his having deserted. On this quarter, therefore, a file of select marksmen was stationed, with directions instantly to pick off every moving figure that showed itself within their range. Of these men, Maximilian himself took the command, and by this means he obtained the opportunity so enviable to one long separated from his mistress, of occasionally conversing with her, and of watching over her safety. In one point he showed a distinguished control over his inclinations; for, much as he had to tell her, and ardently as he longed for communicating with her on various subjects of common interest, he would not suffer her to keep the window down for more than a minute or two in so dreadful a state of the atmosphere. She, on her part, exacted a promise from him that he would leave his station at three o'clock in the morning. Meantime, as on the one hand she felt touched by this proof of her lover's solicitude for her safety, so, on the other, she was less anxious on his account, from the knowledge she had of his long habituation to the hardships of a camp, with which, indeed, he had been familiar from his childish days. Thus debarred from conversing with her lover, and at the same time feeling the most absolute confidence in his protection, she soon fell placidly asleep. The foremost subject of her anxiety and sorrow was now removed; her lover had been restored to her hopes; and her dreams were no longer haunted with horrors. Yet, at the same time, the turbulence of joy and of hope fulfilled unexpectedly, had substituted its own disturbances; and her sleep was often interrupted. But, as often as that happened, she had the delightful pleasure of seeing her lover's figure, with its martial equipments, and the drooping plumes of his yager barrette, as he took his station at her carriage, traced out on the ground in the bright glare of the flambeaux. She awoke, therefore, continually to the sense of restored happiness ; and at length fell finally asleep, to wake no more until the morning trumpet, at the break of day, proclaimed the approaching preparations for the general movement of the camp.

Snow had fallen in the night. Towards four o'clock in the morning, amongst those who held that watch, there had been a strong apprehension that it would fall heavily. But that state of the atmosphere had passed off ;and it had not in fact fallen sufficiently to abate the cold, or much to retard their march. According to the usual custom of the camp, a general breakfast was prepared, at which all without distinction messed together — a sufficient homage being expressed to superior rank by resigning the upper part of every table to those who had any distinguished pretensions of that kind. On this occasion, Paulina had the gratification of seeing the public respect offered in the most marked manner to her lover. He had retired about daybreak to take an hour's repose, — for she found, from her attendants, with mingled vexation and pleasure, that he had not fulfilled his promise of retiring at an earlier hour, in consequence of some renewed appearances of a suspicious kind in the woods. In his absence, she heard a resolution proposed and carried amongst the whole body of veteran officers attached to the party, that the chief military command should be transferred to Maximilian, not merely as a distinguished favorite of the Emperor, but also, and much more, as one of the most brilliant cavalry officers in the Imperial service. This resolution was communicated to him on his taking the place reserved for him, at the head of the principal breakfast-table ; and Paulina thought that he had never appeared more interesting or truly worthy of admiration, than under that exhibition of courtesy and modest dignity with which he first earnestly declined the honor in favor of older officers, — and then finally complied, with what he found to be the sincere wish of the company, by frankly accepting it. Paulina had grown up amongst military men, and had been early trained to a sympathy with military merit — the very court of the Emperor had something of the complexion of a camp — and the object of her own youthful choice was elevated in her eyes, if it were at all possible that he should be so, by this ratification of his claims on the part of those whom she looked up to as the most competent judges.

Before nine o'clock the van of the party was in motion ; then, with a short interval came all the carriages of every description, and the Papenheim dragoons as a rearguard. About eleven, the sun began to burst out, and illuminated, with the cheerful crimson of a frosty morning, those horizontal draperies of mist which had previously stifled his beams. The extremity of the cold was a good deal abated by this time, and Paulina, alighting from her carriage, mounted a led horse, which gave her the opportunity, so much wished for by them both, of conversing freely with Maximilian. For a long time the interest and animation of their reciprocal communications, and the magnitude of the events since they had parted, affecting either or both of them directly, or in the persons of their friends, had the natural effect of banishing any dejection which nearer and more pressing concerns would else have called forth. But, in the midst of this factitious animation, and the happiness which otherwise so undisguisedly possessed Maximilian at their unexpected re-union, it shocked Paulina to observe in her lover a degree of gravity almost amounting to sadness, which argued, in a soldier of his gallantry, some overpowering sense of danger. In fact, upon being pressed to say the worst, Maximilian frankly avowed, that he was ill at ease with regard to their prospects when the hour of trial should arrive ; and that hour he had no hope of evading. Holkerstein, he well knew, had been continually receiving reports of their condition, as they reached their nightly stations, for the last three days. Spies had been round about them, and even in the midst of them, throughout the darkness of the last night. Spies were keeping pace with them as they advanced. The certainty of being attacked was therefore pretty nearly absolute. Then, as to their means of defence, and the relations of strength between the parties, in numbers it was not impossible that Holkerstein might triple themselves. The *élite* of their own men might be superior to most of his, though counting amongst their numbers many deserters from veteran regiments; but the horses of their own party were in general poor and out of condition, — and of the whole train, whom Maximilian had inspected at starting, not two hundred could be pronounced fit for making or sustaining a charge. It was true, that by mounting some of their picked troopers upon the superior horses of the most distinguished amongst the travellers, who had willingly consented to an arrangement of this nature for the general benefit, some partial remedy had been applied to their weakness in that one particular. But there were others in which Holkerstein had even greater advantages; more especially, the equipments of his partisans were entirely new, having been plundered from an ill-guarded armory near Munich, or from convoys which he had attacked. "Who would be a gentleman," says an old proverb, "let him storm a town," and the gay appearance of this robber's companions threw a light upon its meaning. The ruffian companions of this marauder were, besides, animated by hopes such as no regular commander in an honorable service could find the means of holding out. And finally, they were familiar with all the forest roads and innumerable by-paths, on which it was that the best points lay for surprising an enemy, or for a retreat: whilst, in their own case, encumbered with the protection of a large body of travellers and helpless people, whom, under any circumstances, it was hazardous to leave, they were tied up to the most slavish dependency upon the weakness of their companions; and had it not in their power either to evade the most evident advantages on the side of the enemy, or to pursue such as they might be fortunate enough to create for themselves.

"But, after all," said Maximilian, assuming a tone of gayety, upon finding that the candor of his explanations had depressed his fair companion, "the saying of an old Swedish * enemy of mine is worth remembering in such cases, — that nine times out of ten a drachm of good luck is worth an ounce of good contrivance, — and were it not, dearest Paulina, that you are with us, I would think the risk not heavy. Perhaps, by to-morrow's sunset, we shall all look back from our pleasant seats in the warm refectories of Klosterheim, with something of scorn upon our present apprehensions. — And see! at this very moment the turn of the road has brought us in view of our port, though distant from us, according to the windings of the forest, something more than twenty miles. That range of hills, which you observe ahead, but a little inclined to the left, overhangs Klosterheim; and with the sun in a more favorable quarter, you might even at this point descry

* It was the Swedish General Kniphausen, a favorite of Gustavus, to whom this maxim is ascribed.

the pinnacles of the citadel, or the loftiest of the convent towers. Half an hour will bring us to the close of our day's march."

In reality, a few minutes sufficed to bring them within view of the *chateau*, where their quarters had been prepared for this night. This was a great hunting establishment, kept up at vast expense by the two last and present Landgraves of X——. Many interesting anecdotes were connected with the history of this building ; and the beauty of the forest scenery was conspicuous even in winter, enlivened as the endless woods continued to be by the scarlet berries of mountain-ash, or the dark verdure of the holly and the ilex. Under her present frame of pensive feeling, the quiet lawns and long-withdrawing glades of these vast woods, had a touching effect upon the feelings of Paulina ; their deep silence, and the tranquillity which reigned amongst them, contrasting in her remembrance with the hideous scenes of carnage and desolation through which her path had too often lain. With these predisposing influences to aid him, Maximilian found it easy to draw off her attention from the dangers which pressed upon their situation. Her sympathies were so quick with those whom she loved, that she readily adopted their apparent hopes or their fears ; and so entire was her confidence in the superior judgment, and the perfect gallantry of her lover, that her countenance reflected immediately the prevailing expression of his.

Under these impressions Maximilian suffered her to remain. It seemed cruel to disturb her with the truth. He was sensible that continued anxiety, and dreadful or afflicting spectacles, had with her, as with most persons of her sex in Germany at that time, unless protected by singular insensibility, somewhat impaired the firm tone of her mind. He was determined, therefore, to consult her comfort, by disguising or palliating their true situation. But for his own part, he could not hide from his conviction the extremity of their danger; nor could he, when recurring to the precious interests at stake upon the issue of that and the next day's trials, face with any firmness the afflicting results to which they tended, under the known barbarity and ruffian character of their unprincipled enemy.

CHAPTER V.

The chateau of Falkenberg, which the travellers reached with the decline of light, had the usual dependencies of offices and gardens, which may be supposed essential to a prince's hunting establishment in that period. It stood at a distance of eighteen miles from Klosterheim, and presented the sole *oasis* of culture and artificial beauty throughout the vast extent of those wild tracts of sylvan ground.

The great central pile of the building was dismantled of furniture ; but the travellers carried with them, as was usual in the heat of war, all the means of fencing against the cold, and giving even a luxurious equipment to their dormitories. In so large a party, the deficiencies of one were compensated by the redundant contributions of another. And so long as they were not under the old Roman interdict, excluding them from seeking fire and water of those on whom their day's journey had thrown them, their own travelling stores enabled them to accommodate themselves to all other privations. On this occasion, however, they found more than they had expected; for there was at Falkenberg a store of all the game in season, constantly kept up for the use of the Landgrave's household, and the more favored monasteries at Klosterheim. The small establishment of keepers, foresters, and other servants, who occupied the chateau, had received no orders to refuse the hospitality usually practised in the Landgrave's name; or thought proper to dissemble them in their present circumstances of inability to resist. And having from necessity permitted so much, they were led by a sense of their master's honor, or their own sympathy with the condition of so many women and children, to do more. Rations of game were distributed liberally to all the messes; wine was not refused by the old *kellermeister*, who rightly considered that some thanks, and smiles of courteous acknowledgment, might be a better payment than the hard knocks with which military paymasters were sometimes apt to settle their accounts. And upon the whole, it was agreed that no such evening of comfort and even luxurious enjoyment had been spent since their departure from Vienna.

One wing of the chateau was magnificently furnished; this, which of itself was tolerably extensive, had been resigned to the use of Paulina, Maximilian, and others of the military gentlemen, whose manners and deportment seemed to entitle them to superior attentions. Here, amongst many marks of refinement and intellectual culture, there was a library, and a gallery of portraits. In the library, some of the officers had detected sufficient evidences of the Swedish alliances clandestinely maintained by the Landgrave; numbers of rare books, bearing the arms of different Imperial cities, which, in the several campaigns of Gustavus, had been appropriated as they fell in his hands, by way of fair reprisals for the robbery of the whole Palatine library at Heidelberg, had been since transferred (as it thus appeared) to the Landgrave, by purchase or as presents; and on either footing argued a correspondence with the Emperor's enemies, which hitherto he had strenuously disavowed. The picture gallery, it was very probable, had been collected in the same manner. It contained little else than portraits, but these were truly admirable and interesting, being all recent works from the pencil of Vandyke, and composing a series of heads and features the most remarkable for station in the one sex, or for beauty in the other, which that age presented. Amongst them were nearly all the Imperial leaders of distinction, and many of the Swedish. Maximilian and his brother officers took the liveliest pleasure in perambulating this gallery with Paulina, and reviewing with her these fine historical memorials. Out of their joint recollections, or the facts of their personal experience, they were able to supply any defective links in that commentary, which her own knowledge of the Imperial court would have enabled her in so many instances to furnish upon this martial register of the age.

The wars of the Netherlands had transplanted to Germany that stock upon which the camps of the Thirty Years' War were originally raised. Accordingly a smaller gallery, at right angles with the great one, presented a series of portraits from the old Spanish leaders and Walloon partisans. From Egmont and Horn, the Duke of Alva and Parma, down to Spinola, the last of that distinguished school of soldiers, no man of eminence was omitted. Even the worthless and insolent Earl of Leicester, with his gallant nephew — that *ultimus Romanorum* in the rolls of chivalry — were not excluded, though it was pretty evident that a Catholic zeal had presided in forming the collection. For, together with the Prince of Orange and *Henri Quatre*, were to be seen their vile assassins — portrayed with a lavish ostentation of ornament, and enshrined in a frame so gorgeous, as raised them in some degree to the rank of consecrated martyrs.

From these past generations of eminent persons, who retained only a traditional or legendary importance in the eyes of most who were now reviewing them, all turned back with delight to the active spirits of their own day, many of them yet living, and as warm with life and heroic aspirations as their inimitable portraits had represented them. Here was Tilly, the "little corporal," now recently stretched in a soldier's grave, with his wily and inflexible features. Over against him was his great enemy, who had first taught him the hard lesson of retreating, Gustavus Adolphus, with his colossal bust, and "atlantéan shoulders, fit to bear the weight of mightiest monarchies." He also had perished, and too probably by the double crime of assassination and private treason ; but the public glory of his short career was proclaimed in the ungenerous exultations of Catholic Rome from Vienna to Madrid, and the individual heroism in the lamentations of soldiers under every banner which now floated in Europe. Beyond him ran the long line of Imperial generals — from Wallenstein, the magnificent and the imaginative, with Hamlet's infirmity of purpose, De Mercy, &c., down to the heroes of partisan warfare, Holk, the Butlers, and the noble Papenheim, or nobler Piccolómini. Below them were ranged — Gustavus Horn, Banier, the Prince of Saxe-Weimar, the Rhinegrave, and many other Protestant commanders, whose names and military merits were familiar to Paulina, though she now beheld their features for the first time. Maximilian was here the best interpreter that she could possibly have met with. For he had not only seen the greater part of them on the field of battle, but as a favorite and confidential officer of the Emperor's, had personally been concerned in diplomatic transactions with the most distinguished amongst them.

Midnight insensibly surprised them whilst pursuing the many interesting historical remembrances which the portraits called up. Most of the company upon this warning of the advanced hour began to drop off; some to rest, and some upon the summons of the military duty which awaited them in their turn. In this way, Maximilian and Paulina were gradually left alone, and now at length found a time which had not before offered for communicating freely all that pressed upon their hearts. Maximilian, on his part, going back to the period of their last sudden separation, explained his own sudden disappearance from Vienna. At a moment's warning he had been sent off with sealed orders from the Emperor, to be first opened in Klosterheim: the mission upon which he had been despatched was of consequence to the Imperial interests, and through his majesty's favor would eventually prove so to his own. Thus it was that he had been peremptorily cut off from all opportunity of communicating to herself the purpose and direction of his journey previously to his departure from Vienna; and if his majesty had not taken that care upon himself, but had contented himself in the most general terms with assuring Paulina that Maximilian was absent on a private mission, doubtless his intention had been the kind one of procuring her a more signal surprise of pleasure upon his own sudden return. Unfortunately, however, that return had become impossible: things had latterly taken a turn, which embarrassed himself, and continued to require his presence. These perplexities had been for some time known to the Emperor; and upon reflection, he doubted not, that her own journey, undertaken before his Majesty could be aware of the dangers which would beset its latter end, must in some way be connected with the remedy which the Emperor designed for this difficult affair. But doubtless she herself was the bearer of sufficient explanations from the Imperial ministers on that head. Finally, whilst assuring her that his own letters to herself had been as frequent as in any former absence, Maximilian confessed that he did not feel greatly astonished at the fact of none at all having reached her, when he recollected that to the usual adverse accidents of war, daily intercepting all messengers not powerfully escorted, were to be added, in this case, the express efforts of private malignity in command of all the forest passes.

This explanation recalled Paulina to a very painful sense of the critical importance which might be attached to the papers which she had lost. As yet, she had found no special opportunity, or, believing it of less importance, had neglected it, for communicating more than the general fact of a robbery. She now related the case more circumstantially; and both were struck with it, as at this moment a very heavy misfortune. Not only might her own perilous journey, and the whole purposes of the Emperor embarked upon it, be thus rendered abortive ; but their common enemies would by this time be possessed of the whole information which had been so critically lost to their own party, and perhaps would have it in their power to make use of themselves as instruments for defeating their own most important hopes.

Maximilian sighed as he reflected on the probability that a far shorter and bloodier event might defeat every earthly hope within the next twenty-four hours. But he dissembled his feelings ; recovered even a tone of gayety ; and, begging of Paulina to dismiss this vexatious incident from her thoughts, as a matter that after all would probably be remedied by their first communication with the Emperor, and before any evil had resulted from it, he accompanied her to the entrance of her own suite of chambers, and then returned to seek a few hours' repose for himself on one of the sofas he had observed in one of the small ante-rooms attached to the library.

The particular room which he selected for his purpose, on account of its small size, and its warm appearance in other respects, was furnished under foot with layers of heavy Turkey carpets, one laid upon another (according to a fashion then prevalent in Germany), and on the walls with tapestry. In this mode of hanging rooms, though sometimes heavy and sombre, there was a warmth sensible and apparent as well as real, which peculiarly fitted it for winter apartments, and a massy splendor which accorded with the style of dress and furniture in that gorgeous age. One real disadvantage, however, it had as often employed; it gave a ready concealment to intruders with evil intentions; and under the protecting screen of tapestry many a secret had been discovered; many robberies facilitated; and some celebrated murderers had been sheltered, with circumstances of mystery that forever baffled investigation.

Maximilian smiled as the sight of the hangings, with their rich colors glowing in the fire-light, brought back to his remembrance one of those tales which in the preceding winter had made a great noise in Vienna. With a soldier's carelessness, he thought lightly of all dangers that could arise within four walls; and having extinguished the lights which burned upon a table, and unbuckled his sabre, he threw himself upon a sofa which he drew near to the fire; and then enveloping himself in a large horseman's cloak, he courted the approach of sleep. The fatigues of the day, and of the preceding night, had made this in some measure needful to him. But weariness is not always the best preface to repose; and the irritation of many busy anxieties continued for some time to keep him in a most uneasy state of vigilance. As he lay, he could see on one side the fantastic figures in the fire composed of wood and turf; on the other side, looking to the tapestry, he saw the wild forms and the *melée*, little less fantastic, of human and brute features in a chase—a boar chase in front, and a stag chase on his left hand. These, as they rose fitfully in bright masses of color and of savage expression under the lambent flashing of the fire, continued to excite his irritable state of feeling; and it was not for some time that he felt this uneasy condition give way to exhaustion. He was at length on the very point of falling asleep, or perhaps had already fallen into its very lightest and earliest stage, when the echo of a distant door awoke him. He had some slight impression that a noise in his own room had concurred with the other and more distant one to awake him. But, after raising himself for a moment on his elbow and listening, he again resigned himself to sleep.

Again, however, and probably before he had slept a minute, he was roused by a double disturbance. A low rustling was heard in some part of the room, and a heavy foot upon a neighboring staircase. Roused at length to the prudence of paying some attention to sounds so stealthy, in a situation beset with dangers, he rose and threw open the door. A corridor, which ran round the head of the staircase, was lit up with a brilliant light; and he could command from this station one flight of the stairs. On these he saw nothing;

all was now wrapt in a soft effulgence of light, and in absolute silence. No sound recurring after a minute's attention, and indisposed by weariness to any stricter examination, where all examination from one so little acquainted with the localities might prove unavailing, he returned to his own room; but before again lying down, he judged it prudent to probe the concealments of the tapestry by carrying his sabre round, and everywhere pressing the hangings to the wall. In this trial he met with no resistance at any point; and willingly believing that he had been deceived, or that his ear had exaggerated some trivial sound, in a state of imperfect slumber, he again laid down and addressed himself to sleep. Still there were remembrances which occurred at this moment to disturb him. The readiness with which they had been received at the chateau was in itself suspicious. He remembered the obstinate haunting of their camp on the preceding night, and the robbery conducted with so much knowledge of circumstances. Jonas Melk, the brutal landlord of Waldenhausen, a man known to him by repute (though not personally), as one of the vilest agents employed by the Landgrave, had been actively engaged in his master's service at their preceding stage. He was probably one of those who haunted the wood through the night. And he had been repeatedly informed through the course of the day, that this man in particular, whose features were noticed by the yagers, on occasion of their officer's reproach to him, had been seen at intervals in company with others, keeping a road parallel to their own, and steadily watching their order of advance.

These recollections, now laid together, impressed him with some uneasiness. But overpowering weariness gave him a strong interest in dismissing them. And a soldier, with the images of fifty combats fresh in his mind, does not willingly admit the idea of danger from a single arm, and in a situation of household security. Pshaw! he exclaimed, with some disdain, as these martial remembrances rose up before him, especially as the silence had now continued undisturbed for a quarter of an hour. In five minutes more he had fallen profoundly asleep; and in less than one half hour, as he afterwards judged, he was suddenly awakened by a dagger at his throat.

At one bound he sprung upon his feet. The cloak, in which he had been enveloped, caught upon some of the buckles or ornamented work of his appointments, and for a moment embarrassed his motions. There was no light, except what came from the sullen and intermitting gleams of the fire. But even this was sufficient to show him the dusky outline of two figures. With the foremost he grappled, and, raising him in his arms, threw him powerfully upon the floor, with a force that left him stunned and helpless. The other had endeavored to pinion his arms from behind; for the body armor, which Maximilian had not laid aside for the night, under the many anticipations of service which their situation suggested, proved a sufficient protection against the blows of the assassin's poinard. Impatient of the darkness and uncertainty, Maximilian rushed to the door and flung it violently open. The assassin still clung to his arms, conscious that if he once forfeited his hold until he had secured a retreat, he should be taken at disadvantage. But Maximilian now drawing a petronel which hung at his belt, cocked it as rapidly as his embarrassed motions allowed him. The assassin faltered, conscious that a moment's relaxation of grasp would enable his antagonist to turn the muzzle over his shoulder. Maximilian, on the other hand, now perfectly awake, and with the benefit of that self-possession which the other so entirely wanted, felt the nervous tremor in the villain's hands; and profiting by this moment of indecision, made a desperate effort, released one arm, which he used with so much effect as immediately to liberate the other, and then intercepting the passage to the stairs, wheeled round upon his murderous enemy, and presenting the pretronel to his breast, bade him surrender his arms if he hoped for quarter.

The man was an athletic, and, obviously, a most powerful ruffian. On his face he carried more than one large, glazed cicatrix, that assisted the savage expression of malignity impressed by nature upon his features. And his matted black hair, with its elf locks, completed the picturesque effect of a face that proclaimed, in every lineament, a reckless abandonment to cruelty and ferocious passions. Maximilian himself, familiar as he was with the faces of military butchers in the dreadful hours of sack and carnage, recoiled for one instant from this hideous ruffian, who had not even the palliations of youth in his favor, for he seemed fifty at the least. All this had passed in an instant of time, and now, as he recovered himself from his momentary shock at so hateful an expression of evil passions, great was Maximilian's astonishment to perceive his antagonist apparently speechless, and struggling with some over-mastering sense of horror, that convulsed his features, and for a moment glazed his eye.

Maximilian looked around for the object of his alarm, but in vain. In reality it was himself, in connection with some too dreadful remembrances, now suddenly awakened, that had thus overpowered the man's nerves. The brilliant light of a large chandelier, which overhung the staircase, fell strongly upon Maximilian's features, and the excitement of the moment gave to them the benefit of their fullest expression. Prostrate on the ground, and abandoning his dagger without an effort at retaining it, the man gazed, as if under a rattlesnake's fascination, at the young soldier before him. Suddenly he recovered his voice;

and, with a piercing cry of unaffected terror, exclaimed, "Save me, save me, blessed Virgin! — Prince, noble prince, forgive me! — Will the grave not hold its own? — Jesu Maria! who could have believed it?"

"Listen, fellow!" interrupted Maximilian; "what prince is it you speak of? — For whom do you take me? Speak truly, and abuse not my forbearance."

"Ha! and his own voice, too! — and here on this spot! — God is just! — Yet do thou, good patron, holy St. Ermengarde, deliver me from the avenger!"

"Man, you rave! — Stand up, recover yourself, and answer me to what I shall ask thee; speak truly, and thou shalt have thy life. Whose gold was it that armed thy hand against one who had injured neither thee nor thine?"

But he spoke to one who could no longer hear. The man grovelled on the ground, and hid his face from a being whom, in some incomprehensible way, he regarded as an apparition from the other world.

Multitudes of persons had by this time streamed in, summoned by the noise of the struggle from all parts of the chateau. Some fancied that, in the frenzied assassin on the ground, whose panic too manifestly attested itself as genuine, they recognized one of those who had so obstinately dogged them by side-paths in the forest. Whoever he were, and upon whatever mission employed, he was past all rational examination; at the aspect of Maximilian, he relapsed into convulsive horrors, which soon became too fit for medical treatment to allow of any useful judicial inquiry, and for the present he was consigned to the safe keeping of the Provost Marshal.

His companion, meantime, had profited by his opportunity and the general confusion, to effect his escape. Nor was this difficult. Perhaps, in the consternation of the first moment, and the exclusive attention that settled upon the party in the corridor, he might even have mixed in the crowd. But this was not necessary; for, on raising the tapestry, a door was discovered which opened into a private passage, having a general communication with the rest of the rooms on that floor. Steps were now taken, by sentries disposed through the interior of the mansion at proper points, to secure themselves from the enemies who lurked within, whom hitherto they had too much neglected for the avowed and more military assailants who menaced them from without. Security was thus restored. But a deep impression accompanied the party to their couches, of the profound political motives, or (in the absence of those) of the rancorous personal malignity, which could prompt such obstinate persecution; by modes, also, and by hands, which encountered so many chances of failing; and which, even in the event of the very completest success for the present, could not be expected, under the eyes of so many witnesses, to escape a final exposure. Some enemy, of unusual ferocity, was too obviously working in the dark, and by agencies as mysterious as his own purpose.

Meantime, in the city of Klosterheim the general interest in the fortunes of the approaching travellers had suffered no abatement, and some circumstances had occurred to increase the popular irritation. It was known that Maximilian had escaped with a strong party of friends from the city; but how, or by whose connivance, could in no way be discovered. This had drawn upon all persons who were known as active partisans against the Landgrave, or liable to suspicion as friends of Maximilian, a vexatious persecution from the military police of the town. Some had been arrested; many called upon to give security for their future behavior; and all had been threatened or treated with harshness. Hence, as well as from previous irritation and alarm on account of the party from Vienna, the whole town was in a state of extreme agitation.

Klosterheim in the main features of its political distractions, reflected, almost as in a representative picture, the condition of many another German city. At that period, by very ancient ties of reciprocal service, strengthened by treaties, by religious faith, and by personal attachment to individuals of the Imperial house, this ancient and sequestered city was inalienably bound to the interests of the Emperor. Both the city and the university were Catholic. Princes of the

Imperial family, and Papal commisioners, who had secret motives for not appearing at Vienna, had more than once found a hospitable reception within the walls. And, amongst many acts of grace by which the Emperors had acknowledged these services and marks of attachment, one of them had advanced a very large sum of money to the city chest for an indefinite time; receiving in return, as the warmest testimony of confidential gratitude which the city could bestow, that *jus liberi ingressûs* which entitled the Emperor's armies to a free passage at all times, and, in cases of extremity, to the right of keeping the city gates and maintaining a garrison in the citadel. Unfortunately, Klosterheim was not *sui juris*, or on the roll of free cities of the Empire, but of the nature of an appanage in the family of the Landgrave of X——; and this circumstance had produced a double perplexity in the politics of the city; — for the late Landgrave, who had been assassinated in a very mysterious manner upon a hunting party, benefited to the fullest extent both by the political and religious bias of the city — being a personal friend of the Emperor's, a Catholic, amiable in his deportment, and generally beloved by his subjects. But the Prince who had succeeded him in the Landgraviate as the next heir, was everywhere odious for the harshness of his government, no less than for the gloomy austerity of his character; and to Klosterheim, in particular, which had been pronounced by some of the first jurisprudents a female appanage, he presented himself under the additional disadvantages of a very suspicious title and a Swedish bias, too notorious to be disguised. At a time when the religious and political attachments of Europe were brought into collisions so strange, that the foremost auxiliary of the Protestant interest in Germany was really the most distinguished Cardinal in the Church of Rome, it did not appear inconsistent with this strong leaning to the King of Sweden, that the Landgrave was privately known to be a Catholic bigot, who practised the severest penances, and tyrant as he showed himself to all others, grovelled himself as an abject devotee at the feet of a haughty confessor. Amongst the populace of Klosterheim, this feature of his character, confronted with the daily proofs of his entire vassalage to the Swedish interest, passed for the purest hypocrisy; and he had credit for no religion at all with the world at large. But the fact was otherwise. Conscious from the first that he held even the Landgraviate by a slender title (for he was no more than cousin once removed to his immediate predecessor), and that his pretensions upon Klosterheim had separate and peculiar defects, sinking of course with the failure of his claim as Landgrave, but not therefore prospering with its success, — he was aware that none but the most powerful arm could keep his princely cap upon his head. The competitors for any part of his possessions, one and all, had thrown themselves upon the Emperor's protection. This, if no other reason, would have thrown him into the arms of Gustavus Adolphus ; and with this, as it happened, other reasons of local importance had then and since co-operated. Time, as it advanced, brought increase of weight to all these motives. Rumors of a dark and ominous tendency, arising no one knew whence, nor by whom encouraged, pointed injuriously to the past history of the Landgrave, and to some dreadful exposures which were hanging over his head. A lady, at present in obscurity, was alluded to as the agent of redress to others, through her own heavy wrongs ; and these rumors were the more acceptable to the people of Klosterheim, because they connected the impending punishment of the hated Landgrave with the restoration of the Imperial connection ; for it was still insinuated, under every version of these mysterious reports, that the Emperor was the ultimate supporter in the last resort, of the lurking claims now on the point of coming forward to challenge public attention. Under these alarming notices, and fully aware that sooner or later he must be thrown into collision with the Imperial court, the Landgrave had now for some time made up his mind to found a merit with the Swedish chancellor and general officers, by precipitating an uncompromising rupture with his Catholic enemies, and thus to extract the grace of a voluntary act, from what, in fact, he knew to be sooner or later inevitable.

Such was the positive and relative aspect of the several interests which were now struggling in Klosterheim. Desperate measures were contemplated by both parties; and, as opportunities should arise, and proper means should develope themselves, more than one party might be said to stand on the brink of great explosions. Conspiracies were moving in darkness, both in the council of the burghers and of the university. Imperfect notices of their schemes, and sometimes delusive or misleading notices, had reached the Landgrave. The city, the university, and the numerous convents, were crowded to excess with refugees. Malecontents of every denomination and every shade, — emissaries of all the factions which then agitated Germany, — reformado soldiers, laid aside by their original employers, under new arrangements, or from private jealousies of new commanders, — great persons with special reasons for courting a temporary seclusion, and preserving a strict incognito, — misers, who fled with their hoards of gold and jewels to this city of refuge, — desolate ladies, from the surrounding provinces, in search of protection for themselves, or for the honor of their daughters; and (not least distinguished among the many classes of fugitives) prophets and enthusiasts of every description, whom the magnitude of the political events, and their re-

religious origin, so naturally called forth in swarms; — these, and many more, in connection with their attendants, troops, students, and the terrified peasantry, from a circle of forty miles radius around the city as a centre, had swelled the city of Klosterheim, from a total of about seventeen, to six or seven-and-thirty thousand. War, with a slight reserve for the late robberies of Holkerstein, had as yet spared this favored nook of Germany. The great storm had whistled and raved around them; but hitherto none had penetrated the sylvan sanctuary, which on every side invested this privileged city. The ground seemed charmed by some secret spells, and consecrated from intrusion. For the great tempest had often swept directly upon them, and yet still had wheeled off, summoned away by some momentary call, to some remoter attraction. But now at length all things portended, that, if the war should revive in strength after this brief suspension, it would fall with accumulated weight upon this yet unravaged district.

This was the anticipation which had governed the Landgrave's policy in so sternly and barbarously interfering with the generous purposes of the Klosterheimers, for carrying over a safe-conduct to their friends and visitors, when standing on the margin of the forest. The robber Holkerstein, if not expressly countenanced by the Swedes, and secretly nursed up to his present strength by Richelieu, was at any rate embarked upon a system of aggression which would probably terminate in connecting him with one or other of those authentic powers. In any case, he stood committed to a course of continued offence upon the Imperial interests; since in that quarter his injuries and insults were already past forgiveness. The interest of Holkerstein, then, ran in the same channel with that of the Landgrave. It was impolitic to weaken him. It was doubly impolitic to weaken him by a measure which must also weaken the Landgrave; for any deduction from his own military force, or from the means of recruiting it, was in that proportion a voluntary sacrifice of the weight he should obtain with the Swedes on making the junction, which he now firmly counted on, with their forces. But a result which he still more dreaded from the co-operation of the Klosterheimers with the caravan from Vienna, was the probable overthrow of that supremacy in the city, which even now was so nicely balanced in his favor, that a slight reinforcement to the other side would turn the scale against him.

In all these calculations of policy, and the cruel measures by which he supported them, he was guided by the counsels of Luigi Adorni — a subtle Italian, whom he had elevated from the post of a private secretary to that of sole minister for the conduct of state affairs. This man, who covered a temperament of terrific violence with a masque of Venetian dissimulation and the most icy reserve, met with no opposition, unless it were occasionally from Father Anselm, the confessor. He delighted in the refinements of intrigue, and in the most tortuous labyrinths of political manœuvring, purely for their own sakes ; and sometimes defeated his own purposes by mere superfluity of diplomatic subtlety ; which hardly, however, won a momentary concern from him in the pleasure he experienced at having found an undeniable occasion for equal subtlety in unweaving his own webs of deception. He had been confounded by the evasion of Maximilian and his friends from the orders of the Landgrave ; and the whole energy of his nature was bent to the discovery of the secret avenues which had opened the means to this elopement.

There were, in those days, as is well known to German antiquaries, few castles or fortresses of much importance in Germany, which did not communicate by subterraneous passages with the exterior country. In many instances these passages were of surprising extent, first emerging to the light in some secluded spot among rocks or woods, at the distance of two, three, or even four miles. There were cases, even, in which they were carried below the beds of rivers as broad and deep as the Rhine, the Elbe, or the Danube. Sometimes there were several of such communications on different faces of the fortress ; and sometimes each of these branched, at some distance from the building, into separate arms, opening at intervals widely apart. And the uses of such secret communications with the world outside, and beyond a besieging enemy, in a land like Germany, with its prodigious subdivision of independent states and free cities, were far greater than they could have been in any one great continuous principality.

In many fortified places these passages had existed from the middle ages. In Klosterheim they had possibly as early an origin; but by this period it is very probable that the gradual accumulation of rubbish, through a course of centuries, would have unfitted them for use, had not the Peasants' War, in the time of Luther's Reformation, little more than one hundred years before, given occasion for their use and repair. At that time Klosterheim had stood a siege, which, from the defect of artillery, was at no time formidable in a military sense; but as a blockade, formed suddenly when the citizens were slenderly furnished with provisions, it would certainly have succeeded, and delivered up the vast wealth of the convents as a spoil to the peasantry, had it not been for one in particular of these subterraneous passages, which opening on the opposite side of the little river Iltiss, in a thick *boccage*, where the enemy had established no posts, furnished the means of introducing a continual supply of fresh provisions, to the great triumph of the garrison, and the utter dismay of the superstitious peasants, who looked upon the mysterious supply as a providential bounty to a consecrated cause.

So memorable a benefit had given to this one passage a publicity and an historical importance which made all its circumstances, and amongst those its internal mouth, familiar even to children. But this was evidently *not* the avenue by which Maximilian had escaped into the forest. For it opened externally on the wrong side of the river, whilst everybody knew that its domestic opening was in one of the chapels of the *schloss ;* and another circumstance equally decisive was, that a long flight of stairs, by which it descended below the bed of the river, made it impassable to horses.

Every attempt, however, failed to trace out the mode of egress for the present. By his spies, Adorni doubted not to find it soon ; and in the meantime, that as much as possible the attention of the public might be abstracted from the travellers and their concerns, a public proclamation was issued forbidding all resorts of crowds to the walls. These were everywhere dispersed on the 9th ; and for that day were partially obeyed. But there was little chance that, with any fresh excitement to the popular interest, they would continue to command respect.

CHAPTER VI.

The morning of the 10th at length arrived — that day on which the expected travellers from Vienna, and all whom they had collected on their progress, ardently looked to rejoin their long separated friends in Klosterheim, and by those friends were not less ardently looked for. On each side there were the same violent yearnings; on each side the same dismal and overpowering fears. Each party arose with palpitating hearts: the one looked out from Falkenberg with longing eyes to discover the towers of Klosterheim; the other, from the upper windows or roofs of Klosterheim, seemed as if they could consume the distance between themselves and Falkenberg. But a little tract of forest ground was interposed between friends and friends, parents and children, lovers and their beloved. Not more than eighteen miles of shadowy woods, of lawns, and sylvan glades, divided hearts that would either have encountered death or many deaths for the other. These were regions of natural peace and tranquillity, that in any ordinary times should have been peopled by no worse inhabitants than the timid hare scudding homewards to its form, or the wild deer sweeping by with thunder to their distant lairs. But now from every glen or thicket armed marauders might be ready to start. Every gleam of sunshine in some seasons was reflected from the glittering arms of parties threading the intricacies of the thickets; and the sudden alarum of the trumpet rang oftentimes in the nights, and awoke the echoes that for centuries had been undisturbed except by the hunter's horn, in the most sequestered haunts of these vast woods.

Towards noon it became known, by signals that had been previously concerted between Maximilian and his college friends, that the party were advanced upon their road from Falkenberg, and therefore must of necessity on this day abide the final trial. As this news was dispersed abroad, the public anxiety rose to so feverish a point, that crowds rushed from every quarter to the walls; and it was not judged prudent to measure the civic strength against their enthusiasm. For an hour or two the nature of the ground and the woods forbade any view of the advancing party: but at length, some time before the light failed, the head of the column, and soon after the entire body, was descried surmounting a little hill not more than eight miles distant. The black mass, presented by mounted travellers and baggage wagons, was visible to piercing eyes: and the dullest could distinguish the glancing of arms which at times flashed upwards from the more open parts of the forest.

Thus far, then, their friends had made their way without injury: and this point was judged to be within nine miles distance. But in thirty or forty minutes, when they had come nearer by a mile and a half, the scene had somewhat changed. A heathy tract of ground, perhaps two miles in length, opened in the centre of the thickest woods, and formed a little island of clear ground where all beside was tangled and crowded with impediments. Just as the travelling party began to deploy out of the woods upon this area at its further extremity, a considerable body of mounted troops emerged from the forest, which had hitherto concealed them, at the point nearest to Klosterheim. They made way rapidly; and in less than half a minute it became evident, by the motions of the opposite party, that they had been descried, and that hasty preparations were making for receiving them. A dusky mass, probably the Black Yagers, galloped up rapidly to the front and formed: after which it seemed to some eyes that the whole party again advanced, but still more slowly than before.

Every heart upon the walls of Klosterheim palpitated with emotion, as the two parties neared each other. Many almost feared to draw their breath, many writhed their persons in the anguish of rueful expectation, as they saw the moment approach when the two parties would shock together. At length it came; and to the astonishment of the spectators, not more perhaps than of the travellers themselves, the whole cavalcade of strangers swept by, without halting for so much as a passing salute or exchange of news.

The first cloud, then, which had menaced their friends, was passed off as suddenly as it had gathered. But this by some people was thought to bear no favorable construction. To ride past a band of travellers from remote parts on such uncourteous terms argued no friendly spirit; and many motives might be imagined perfectly consistent with hostile intentions for passing the travellers unassailed, and thus gaining the means of coming at any time upon their rear. Prudent persons shook their heads; and the issue of an affair anticipated with so much anxiety certainly did not diminish it.

It was now four o'clock: and in an hour or less it would be dark; and, considering the peculiar difficulties of the ground on nearing the town, and the increasing exhaustion of the horses, it was not judged possible that a party of travellers, so unequal in their equipments, and amongst whom the weakest was now become a law for the motion of the quickest, could reach the gates of Klosterheim before nine o'clock.

Soon after this, and just before the daylight faded, the travellers reached the nearer end of the heath, and again entered the woods. The cold and the darkness were now becoming greater at every instant, and it might have been expected that the great mass of the spectators would leave their station ; but such was the intensity of the public interest, that few quitted the walls except for the purpose of reinforcing their ability to stay and watch the progress of their friends. This could be done with even greater effect as the darkness deepened, for every second horseman carried a torch ; and as much perhaps by way of signal to their friends in Klosterheim, as for their own convenience, prodigious flambeaux were borne aloft on halberds. These rose to a height which surmounted all the lower bushes, and were visible in all parts of the woods, — even the smaller lights, in the leafless state of the trees at this season of the year, could be generally traced without difficulty ; and composing a brilliant chain of glittering points, as it curved and humored the road amongst the labyrinths of the forest, would have produced a singularly striking effect to eyes at leisure to enjoy it.

In this way, for about three hours, the travellers continued to advance unmolested, and to be traced by their friends in Klosterheim. It was now considerably after seven o'clock, and perhaps an hour, or at most an hour and a half, would bring them to the city gates. All hearts began to beat high with expectation, and hopes were loudly and confidently expressed through every part of the crowd that the danger might now be considered as past. Suddenly, as if expressly to rebuke the too presumptuous confidence of those who were thus thoughtlessly sanguine, the blare of a trumpet was heard from a different quarter of the forest, and about two miles to the right of the city. Every eye was fastened eagerly upon the spot from which the notes issued. Probably the signal had proceeded from a small party in advance of a greater; for in the same direction, but at a much greater distance, perhaps not less than three miles in the rear of the trumpet, a very large body of horse was now descried coming on at a great pace upon the line already indicated by the trumpet. The extent of the column might be estimated by the long array of torches, which were carried apparently by every fourth or fifth man; and that they were horsemen, was manifest from the very rapid pace at which they advanced.

At this spectacle a cry of consternation ran along the whole walls of Klosterheim. Here then at last were coming the spoilers and butchers of their friends; for the road upon which they were advancing issued at right angles into that upon which the travellers, apparently unwarned of their danger, were moving. The hideous scene of carnage would possibly pass immediately below their own eyes; for the point of junction between the two roads was directly commanded by the eye from the city walls; and upon computing the apparent proportions of speed between the two parties, it seemed likely enough that upon this very ground, the best fitted of any that could have been selected, in a scenical sense, as a stage for bringing a spectacle below the eyes of Klosterheim, the most agitating of spectacles would be exhibited, — friends and kinsmen engaged in mortal struggle with remorseless free-booters, under circumstances which denied to themselves any chance of offering assistance.

Exactly at this point of time arose a dense mist, which wrapped the whole forest in darkness, and withdrew from the eyes of the agitated Klosterheimers friends and foes alike. They continued, however, to occupy the walls, endeavoring to penetrate the veil which now concealed the fortunes of their travelling friends, by mere energy and intensity of attention. The mist, meantime, did not disperse, but rather continued to deepen: the two parties, however, gradually drew so much nearer, that some judgment could be at length formed of their motions and position merely by the ear. From the stationary character of the sounds, and the continual recurrence of charges and retreats sounded upon the trumpet, it became evident that the travellers and the enemy had at length met, and too probable that they were engaged in a sanguinary combat. Anxiety had now reached its utmost height; and some were obliged to leave the walls, or were carried away by their friends, under the effects of overwrought sensibility.

Ten o'clock had now struck, and for some time the sounds had been growing sensibly weaker, and at last it was manifest that the two parties had separated, and that one at least was moving off from the scene of action; and, as the sounds grew feebler and feebler, there could be no doubt that it was the enemy who was drawing off into the distance from the field of battle.

The enemy! ay, but how? Under what circumstances? As victor? Perhaps even as the captor of their friends? Or, if not, and he were really retreating as a fugitive and beaten foe, with what hideous sacrifices on the part of their friends might not that result have been purchased?

Long and dreary was the interval before these questions could be answered. Full three hours had elapsed since the last sound of a trumpet had been heard: it was now one o'clock, and as yet no trace of the travellers had been discovered in any quarter. The most hopeful began to despond, and general lamentations prevailed throughout Klosterheim.

Suddenly, however, a dull sound arose within a quarter of a mile from the city gate, as of some feeble attempt to blow a blast upon a trumpet. In five minutes more a louder blast was sounded close to the gate. Questions were joyfully put, and as joyfully answered. The usual precautions were rapidly gone through; and the officer of the watch being speedily satisfied as to the safety of the measure, the gates were thrown open, and the unfortunate travellers, exhausted by fatigue, hardships, and suffering of every description, were at length admitted into the bosom of a friendly town.

The spectacle was hideous which the long cavalcade exhibited as it wound up the steep streets which led to the market-place. Wagons fractured and splintered in every direction, upon which were stretched numbers of gallant soldiers, with wounds hastily dressed, from which the blood had poured in streams over their gay habiliments; horses, whose limbs had been mangled by the sabre; and coaches or caleches loaded with burthens of dead and dying; these were amongst the objects which occupied the van in the line of march, as the travellers defiled through Klosterheim. The vast variety of faces, dresses, implements of war, or ensigns of rank, thrown together in the confusion of night and retreat, illuminated at intervals by bright streams of light from torches or candles in the streets, or at the windows of the houses, composed a picture which resembled the chaos of a dream, rather than any ordinary spectacle of human life.

In the market-place the whole party were gradually assembled, and there it was intended that they should receive the billets for their several quarters. But such was the pressure of friends and relatives gathering from all directions, to salute and welcome the objects of their affectionate anxiety, or to inquire after their fate; so tumultuous was the conflict of grief and joy, (and not seldom in the very same group), that for a long time no authority could control the violence of public feeling, or enforce the arrangements which had been adopted for the night. Nor was it even easy to learn, where the questions were put by so many voices at once, what had been the history of the night. It was at length, however, collected, that they had been met and attacked with great fury by Holkerstein, or a party acting under one of his lieutenants. Their own march had been so warily conducted after nightfall, that this attack did not find them unprepared. A barrier of coaches and wagons had been speedily formed in such an arrangement as to cripple the enemy's movements, and to neutralize great part of his superiority in the quality of his horses. The engagement, however, had been severe; and the enemy's attack, though many times baffled, had been as often renewed, until at length, the young general Maximilian, seeing that the affair tended to no apparent termination, that the bloodshed was great, and that the horses were beginning to knock up under the fatigue of such severe service, had brought up the very *élite* of his reserve, placed himself at their head, and making a dash expressly at their leader, had the good fortune to cut him down. The desperateness of the charge, added to the loss of their leader, had intimidated the enemy, who now began to draw off as from an enterprise which was likely to cost them more blood than a final success could have rewarded. Unfortunately, however, Maximilian, disabled by a severe wound, and entangled by his horse amongst the enemy, had been carried off a prisoner. In the course of the battle, all their torches had been extinguished; and this circumstance, as much as the roughness of the road, the ruinous condition of their carriages and appointments, and their own exhaustion, had occasioned their long delay in reaching Klosterheim, after the battle was at an end. Signals they had not ventured to make; for they were naturally afraid of drawing upon their track any fresh party of marauders by so open a warning of their course as the sound of a trumpet.

These explanations were rapidly dispersed through Klosterheim; party after party drew off to their quarters; and at length the agitated city was once again restored to peace. The Lady Paulina had been amongst the first to retire. She was met by the Lady Abbess of a principal convent in Klosterheim, to whose care she had been recommended by the Emperor. The Landgrave also had furnished her with a guard of honor; but all expressions of respect, or even of kindness, seemed thrown away upon her, so wholly was she absorbed in grief for the capture of Maximilian, and in gloomy anticipations of his impending fate.

CHAPTER VII.

THE city of Klosterheim was now abandoned to itself, and strictly shut up within its own walls. All roaming beyond those limits was now indeed forbidden even more effectually by the sword of the enemy than by the edicts of the Landgrave. War was manifestly gathering in its neighborhood. Little towns and castles within a range of seventy miles, on almost every side, were now daily occupied by Imperial or Swedish troops. Not a week passed without some news of fresh military accessions, or of skirmishes between parties of hostile foragers. Through the adjacent country, spite of the severe weather, bodies of armed men were weaving to and fro, fast as a weaver's shuttle. The forest rang with alarums, and sometimes under gleams of sunshine, the leafless woods seemed on fire with the restless splendor of spear and sword, morion and breastplate, or the glittering equipments of the Imperial cavalry. Couriers, or Bohemian gipsies, which latter were a class of people at this time employed by all sides as spies or messengers, continually stole in with secret despatches to the Landgrave, or (under the color of bringing public news, and the reports of military movements) to execute some private mission for rich employers in town; sometimes making even this clandestine business but a cover to other purposes, too nearly connected with treason, or reputed treason, to admit of any but oral communication.

What were the ulterior views in this large accumulation of military force, no man pretended to know. A great battle, for various reasons, was not expected. But changes were so sudden, and the counsels of each day so often depended on the accidents of the morning, that an entire campaign might easily be brought on, or the whole burthen of war for years to come might be transferred to this quarter of the land, without causing any very great surprise. Meantime, enough was done already to give a full foretaste of war and its miseries to this sequestered nook — so long unvisited by that hideous scourge.

In the forest, where the inhabitants were none, excepting those who lived upon the borders, and small establishments of the Landgrave's servants at different points, for executing the duties of the forest or the chase, this change expressed itself chiefly by the tumultuous uproar of the wild deer, upon whom a murderous war was kept up by parties detached daily from remote and opposite quarters to collect provisions for the half-starving garrisons, so recently, and with so little previous preparation, multiplied on the forest skirts. For though the country had been yet unexhausted by war, too large a proportion of the tracts adjacent to the garrisons were in a wild sylvan condition, to afford any continued supplies to so large and sudden an increase of the population; more especially as, under the rumors of this change, every walled town in a compass of one hundred miles, many of them capable of resisting a sudden *coup-de-main,* and resolutely closing their gates upon either party, had already possessed themselves by purchase of all the surplus supplies which the country yielded. In such a state of things, the wild deer became an object of valuable consideration to all parties, and a murderous war was made upon them from every side of the forest. From the city walls they were seen in sweeping droves, flying before the Swedish cavalry for a course of ten, fifteen, or even thirty miles, until headed, and compelled to turn by another party breaking suddenly from a covert where they had been waiting their approach. Sometimes it would happen that this second party proved to be a body of Imperialists, who were carried by the ardor of the chase into the very centre of their enemies before either was aware of any hostile approach. Then, according to circumstances, came sudden flight or tumultuary skirmish; the woods rang with the hasty summons of the trumpet; the deer reeled off aslant from the furious shock, and benefiting for the moment by those fierce hostilities, originally the cause of their persecution, fled far away from the scene of strife; and not unfrequently came thundering beneath the city walls, and reporting to the spectators above, by their agitation and affrighted eyes, those tumultuous disturbances in some remoter part of the forest, which had already reached them in an imperfect way, by the interrupted and recurring echoes of the points of war — charges or retreats — sounded upon the trumpet.

But, whilst on the outside of her walls Klosterheim beheld this unpopulous region all alive with military license and outrage, she suffered no violence from either party herself. This immunity she owed to her peculiar political situation. The Emperor had motives for conciliating the city; the Swedes for conciliating the Landgrave: indeed they were supposed to have made a secret alliance with him, for purposes known only to the contracting parties. And the difference between the two patrons was simply this, that the Emperor was sincere, and, if not disinterested, had an interest concurring with that of Klosterheim, in the paternal protection which he offered; whereas the Swedes in this, as in all their arrangements, regarding Germany as a foreign country, looked only to the final advantages of Sweden or its German dependencies, and to the weight with such alliances would procure them in a general pacification. And hence, in the war which both combined to make upon the forest, the one party professed to commit spoil upon the Landgrave, as distinguished from the city; whilst the Swedish allies of that prince prosecuted their ravages in the Landgrave's name, as essential to the support of his cause.

For the present, however, the Swedes were the preponderant party in the neighborhood; they had fortified the chateau of Falkenberg, and made it a very strong military post; at the same time, however, sending in to Klosterheim whatsoever was valuable amongst the furniture of that establishment, with a care which of itself proclaimed the footing upon which they were anxious to stand with the Landgrave.

Encouraged by the vicinity of his military friends, that Prince now began to take a harsher tone in Klosterheim. The minor princes of Germany at that day were all tyrants in virtue of their privileges; and if in some rarer cases they exercised these privileges in a forbearing spirit, their subjects were well aware that they were indebted for this extraordinary indulgence to the temper and gracious nature of the individual, not to the firm protection of the laws. But the most reasonable and mildest of the German princes had been little taught at that day to brook opposition; and the Landgrave was by nature, and the gloominess of his constitutional temperament, of all men the last to learn that lesson readily. He had already met with just sufficient opposition from the civic body and the university interest to excite his passion for revenge. Ample indemnification he determined upon for his wounded pride; and he believed that the time and circumstances were now matured for favoring his most vindictive schemes. The Swedes were at hand; and a slight struggle with the citizens would remove all obstacles to their admission into the garrison; though, for some private reasons, he wished to abstain from this extremity, if it should prove possible. Maximilian also was absent, and might never return. The rumor was even that he was killed; and though the caution of Adorni and the Landgrave led them to a hesitating reliance upon what might be a political fabrication of the opposite party, yet at all events he was detained from Klosterheim by some pressing necessity; and the period of his absence, whether long or short, the Landgrave resolved to improve in such a way as should make his return unavailing.

Of Maximilian the Landgrave had no personal knowledge; he had not so much as seen him. But by his spies and intelligencers he was well aware that he had been the chief combiner and animater of the Imperial party against himself in the university, and by his presence had given life and confidence to that party in the city which did not expressly acknowledge him as their head. He was aware of the favor which Maximilian enjoyed with the Emperor, and knew in general, from public report, the brilliancy of those military services on which it had been built. That he was likely to prove a formidable opponent, had he continued in Klosterheim, the Landgrave knew too well; and upon the advantage over him which he had now gained, though otherwise it should prove only a temporary one, he determined to found a permanent obstacle to the Emperor's views. As a preliminary stêp, he prepared to crush all opposition in Klosterheim; a purpose which was equally important to his vengeance and his policy.

This system he opened with a series of tyrannical regulations, some of which gave the more offence that they seemed wholly capricious and insulting. The students were confined to their college bounds, except at stated intervals; were subject to a military muster, or calling over of names, every evening; were required to receive sentinels within the extensive courts of their own college, and at length a small court of guard; with numerous other occasional marks, as opportunities offered, of princely discountenance and anger.

In the university, at that time, from local causes, many young men of rank and family were collected. Those even, who had taken no previous part in the cause of the Klosterheimers, were now roused to a sense of personal indignity. And as soon as the light was departed, a large body of them collected at the rooms of Count St. Aldenheim, whose rank promised a suitable countenance to their purpose, whilst his youth seemed a pledge for the requisite activity.

The Count was a younger brother of the Palsgrave of Birkenfeld, and maintained a sumptuous establishment in Klosterheim. Whilst the state of the forest had allowed of hunting, hawking, or other amusements, no man had exhibited so fine a stud of horses. No man had so large a train of servants; no man entertained his friends with such magnificent hospitalities. His generosity, his splendor, his fine person, and the courtesy with which he relieved the humblest people from the oppression of his rank, had given him a popularity amongst the students. His courage had been tried in battle: but, after all, it was doubted whether he were not of too luxurious a turn to undertake any cause which called for much exertion; for the death of a rich Abbess, who had left the whole of an immense fortune to the Count, as her favorite nephew, had given him another motive for cultivating peaceful pursuits, to which few men were, constitutionally, better disposed.

It was the time of day when the Count was sure to be found at home with a joyous party of friends. Magnificent chandeliers shed light upon a table furnished with every description of costly wines produced in Europe. According to the custom of the times, these were drunk in cups of silver or gold; and an opportunity was thus gained, which St. Aldenheim had not lost, of making a magnificent display of luxury without ostentation. The ruby wine glittered in the jewelled goblet which the Count had raised to his lips, at the very moment when the students entered.

"Welcome, friends," said the Count St. Aldenheim, putting down his cup, "welcome always; but never more than at this hour, when wine and good fellowship teach us to know the value of our youth."

"Thanks, Count, from all of us. But the fellowship we seek at present must be of another temper; our errand is of business."

"Then, friends, it shall rest until to-morrow. Not for the papacy, to which my good aunt would have raised a ladder for me of three steps,—Abbot, Bishop, Cardinal, would I renounce the Tokay of to-night for the business of to-morrow. Come, gentlemen, let us drink my aunt's health.

"Memory, you would say, Count."

"Memory, most learned friend, you are right; Ah! gentlemen, she was a woman worthy to be had in remembrance: for she invented a capital plaster for gunshot wounds; and a jollier old fellow over a bottle of Tokay there is not at this day in Suabia, or in the Swedish camp. And that reminds me to ask, gentlemen, have any of you heard that Gustavus Horn is expected at Falkenberg? Such news is astir; and be sure of this — that in such a case, we have cracked crowns to look for. I know the man. And many a hard night's watching he has cost me; for which, if you please, gentlemen, we will drink his health."

"But our business, dear Count —"

"Shall wait, please God, until to-morrow; for this is the time when man and beast repose."

"And truly, Count, weare like — as you take things — to be numbered with the last. Fie, Count St. Aldenheim! are you the man that would have us suffer those things tamely which the Landgrave has begun?"

"And what now hath his Serenity been doing? Doth he meditate to abolish burgundy? If so, my faith! but we are, as you observe, little above the brutes. Or, peradventure, will he forbid laughing — his Highness being little that way given himself?"

"Count St. Aldenheim it pleases you to jest. But we are assured that you know as well as we, and relish no better, the insults which the Landgrave is heaping upon us all. For example, the sentinel at your own door — doubtless you marked him? How liked you him?"

"Methought he looked cold and blue. So I sent him a goblet of Johannisberg."

"You did? and the little court of guard — you have seen *that*? and Colonel Von Aremberg, how think you of him?"

"Why surely now he's a handsome man: pity he

wears so fiery a scarf! Shall we drink his health, gentlemen?"

"Health to the great fiend first!"

"As you please, gentlemen: it is for you to regulate the precedency. But at least,

> "Here's to my aunt—the jolly old sinner,
> That fasted each day, from breakfast to dinner!
> Saw any man yet such an orthodox fellow,
> In the morning when sober, in the evening when mellow?
> Saw any man yet," &c.

"Count, farewell!"—interrupted the leader of the party; and all turned round indignantly to leave the room.

"Farewell, gentleman, as you positively will not drink my aunt's health; though, after all, she was a worthy fellow; and her plaster for gunshot wounds,—"

But with that word the door closed upon the Count's farewell words. Suddenly taking up a hat which lay upon the ground, he exclaimed, "Ah! behold! one of my friends has left his hat. Truly he may chance to want it on a frosty night." And, so saying, he hastily rushed after the party, whom he found already on the steps of the portico. Seizing the hand of the leader, he whispered,—

"Friend! do you know me so little, as to apprehend my jesting in a serious sense? Know that two of those, whom you saw on my right hand, are spies of the Landgrave? Their visit to me, I question not, was purposely made to catch some such discoveries as you, my friends, would too surely have thrown in their way, but for my determined rattling. At this time, I must not stay. Come again after midnight — farewell."

And then in a voice to reach his guests within, he shouted, "Gentlemen, my aunt, the Abbot of Ingelheim, — Abbess, I would say, held that her spurs were for her heels, and her beaver for her head. Whereupon, Baron, I return you your hat."

Meantime, the two insidious intelligencers of the Landgrave returned to the palace with discoveries, not so ample as they were on the point of surprising, but sufficient to earn thanks for themselves, and to guide the counsels of their masters.

CHAPTER VIII.

THAT same night a full meeting of the most distinguished students was assembled at the mansion of Count St. Aldenheim. Much stormy discussion arose upon two points; first, upon the particular means by which they were to pursue an end upon which all were unanimous. Upon that, however, they were able for the present to arrive at a preliminary arrangement with sufficient harmony. This was, to repair in a body, with Count St. Aldenheim at their head, to the castle, and there to demand an audience of the Landgrave, at which a strong remonstrance was to be laid before his highness, and their determination avowed to repel the indignities thrust upon them, with their united forces. On the second they were more at variance. It happened that many of the persons present, and amongst them Count St. Aldenheim, were friends of Maximilian. A few, on the other hand, there were, who, either from jealousy of his distinguished merit, hated him; or as good citizens of Klosterheim, and connected by old family ties with the interests of that town, were disposed to charge Maximilian with ambitious views of private aggrandizement at the expense of the city, grounded upon the Emperor's favor, or upon a supposed marriage with some lady of the Imperial house. For the story of Paulina's and Maximilian's mutual attachment had transpired through many of the travellers ; but with some circumstances of fiction. In defending Maximilian upon those charges, his friends had betrayed a natural warmth at the injustice offered to his character ; and the liveliness of the dispute on this point, had nearly ended in a way fatal to their unanimity on the immediate question at issue. Good sense, however, and indignation at the Landgrave, finally brought them round again to their first resolution ; and they separated with the unanimous intention of meeting at noon on the following day, for the purpose of carrying it into effect.

But their unanimity on this point was of little avail ; for at an early hour on the following morning, every one of those who had been present at the meeting, was arrested by a file of soldiers on a charge of conspiracy, and marched off to one of the city prisons. The Count St. Aldenheim was himself the sole exception ; and this was a distinction odious to his generous nature, as it drew upon him a cloud of suspicion. He was sensible that he would be supposed to owe his privilege to some discovery or act of treachery, more or less, by which he had merited the favor of the Landgrave. The fact was, that in the indulgence shown to the Count, no motive had influenced the Landgrave but a politic consideration of the great favor and influence which the Count's brother, the Palsgrave, at this moment enjoyed in the camp of his own Swedish allies. On this principle of policy, the Landgrave contented himself with placing St. Aldenheim under a slight military confinement to his own house, under the guard of a few sentinels posted in his hall.

For *him*, therefore, under the powerful protection which he enjoyed elsewhere, there was no great anxiety entertained. But for the rest, many of whom had no friends, or friends who did them the ill service of enemies, being in fact regarded as enemies by the Landgrave and his council, serious fears were entertained by the whole city. Their situation was evidently critical. The Landgrave had them in his power. He was notoriously a man of gloomy and malignant passions; had been educated, as all European princes then were, in the notions of a plenary and despotic right over the lives of his subjects, in any case where they lifted their presumptious thoughts to the height of controlling their sovereign; and, even in circumstances which to his own judgment might seem to confer much less discretionary power over the rights of prisoners, he had been suspected of directing the course of law and of punishment into channels that would not brook the public knowledge. Darker dealings were imputed to him in the popular opinion. Gloomy suspicions were muttered at the fireside, which no man dared openly to avow ; and in the present instance the conduct of the Landgrave was every way fitted to fall in with the worst of the public fears. At one time he talked of bringing his prisoners to a trial ; at another, he countermanded the preparations which he had made with that view. Sometimes he spoke of banishing them in a body ; and again he avowed his intention to deal with their crime as treason. The result of this moody and capricious tyranny was to inspire the most vague and gloomy apprehensions into the minds of the prisoners, and to keep their friends, with the whole city of Klosterheim, in a feverish state of insecurity.

This state of things lasted for nearly three weeks ; but at length a morning of unexpected pleasure dawned upon the city. The prisoners were in one night all released. In half an hour the news ran over the town and the university ; multitudes hastened to the college, anxious to congratulate the prisoners on their deliverance from the double afflictions of a dungeon and of continual insecurity. Mere curiosity also prompted some, who took but little interest in the prisoners or their cause, to inquire into the circumstances of so abrupt and unexpected an act of grace. One principal court in the college was filled with those who had come upon this errand of friendly interest or curiosity. Nothing was to be seen but earnest and delighted faces, offering or acknowledging congratulation ; nothing to be heard but the language of joy and pleasure — friendly or affectionate, according to the sex or relation of the speaker. Some were talking of procuring passports for leaving the town — some anticipating that this course would not be left to their own choice, but imposed, as the price of his clemency, by the Landgrave ; — all, in short, was hubbub and joyous uproar, when suddenly a file of the city guard, commanded by an officer, made their way rudely and violently through the crowd, advancing evidently to the spot where the liberated prisoners were collected in a group. At that moment the Count St. Aldenheim was offering his congratulations. The friends to whom he spoke, were too confident in his honor and integrity to have felt even one moment's misgiving upon the true causes which had sheltered him from the Landgrave's wrath, and had thus given him a privilege so invidious in the eyes of those who knew him not, and on that account so hateful in his own. They knew his unimpeachable fidelity to the cause and themselves, and were anxiously expressing their sense of it by the warmth of their salutations at the very moment when the city guard appeared. The Count, on his part, was gaily reminding them to come that evening and fulfil their engagement to drink his aunt of jovial memory in her own Johannisberg, when the guard, shouldering aside the crowd, advanced, and, surrounding the group of students, in an instant laid the hands of summary arrest each upon the gentleman who stood next him. The petty officer who commanded, made a grasp at one of the most distinguished in dress, and seized rudely upon the gold chain depending from his neck. St. Aldenheim, who happened at the moment to be in conversation with this individual, stung with a sudden indignation at the ruffian eagerness of the men in thus abusing the privileges of their office, and unable to control the generous ardor of his nature, met this brutal outrage with a sudden blow at the officer's face, levelled with so true an aim, that it stretched him at his length upon the ground. No terrors of impending vengeance, had they been a thousand times stronger than they were, could at this moment have availed to stifle the cry of triumphant pleasure — long, loud, and unfaltering — which indignant sympathy with the oppressed extorted from the crowd. The pain and humiliation of the blow, exalted into a maddening intensity by this popular shout of exultation, quickened the officer's rage into an apparent frenzy. With white lips, and half suffocated with the sudden revulsion of passion, natural enough to one who had never before encountered even a momentary overture at opposition to the authority with which he was armed, and for the first time in his life found his own brutalities thrown back resolutely in his teeth, the man rose, and by signs rather than the inarticulate sounds which he meant for words, pointed the violence of his party upon the

Count St. Aldenheim. With halberds bristling around him, the gallant young nobleman was loudly summoned to surrender; but he protested indignantly, drawing his sword, and placing himself in an attitude of defence, that he would die a thousand deaths sooner than surrender the sword of his father, the Palsgrave, a Prince of the Empire, of unspotted honor, and most ancient descent, into the hands of a jailer.

"Jailer!" exclaimed the officer, almost howling with passion.

"Why, then, captain of jailers, lieutenant, anspessade, or what you will. What else than a jailer is he, that sits watch upon the prison-doors of honorable cavaliers?" Another shout of triumph applauded St. Aldenheim; for the men who discharged the duties of the city guard at that day, or "petty guard," as it was termed, corresponding in many of their functions to the modern police, were viewed with contempt by all parties; and most of all by the military, though in some respects assimilated to them by discipline and costume. They were industriously stigmatized as jailers; for which there was the more ground, as their duties did in reality associate them pretty often with the jailer; and in other respects they were a dissolute and ferocious body of men, gathered not out of the citizens, but many foreign deserters, or wretched runagates from the jail, or from the justice of the Provost Marshal in some distant camp. Not a man, probably, but was liable to be reclaimed in some or other quarter of Germany as a capital delinquent. Sometimes, even, they were actually detected, claimed, and given up to the pursuit of justice, when it happened that the subjects of their criminal acts were weighty enough to sustain an energetic inquiry. Hence their reputation became worse than scandalous; the mingled infamy of their calling, and the houseless condition of wretchedness which had made it worth their acceptance, combined to overwhelm them with public scorn; and this public abhorrence, which at any rate awaited them, mere desperation led them too often to countenance and justify by their conduct.

"Captain of jailers! do your worst, I say," again ejaculated St. Aldenheim. Spite of his blinding passion, the officer hesitated to precipitate himself into a personal struggle with the Count, and thus perhaps afford his antagonist an occasion for a further triumph. But loudly and fiercely he urged on his followers to attack him. These again, not partaking in the personal wrath of their leader, even whilst pressing more and more closely upon St. Aldenheim, and calling upon him to surrender, scrupled to inflict a wound, or too marked an outrage, upon a cavalier whose rank was known to the whole city, and of late most advantageously known for his own interests, by the conspicuous immunity which it had procured him from the Landgrave. In vain did the commanding officer insist, in vain did the Count defy, — menaces from neither side availed to urge the guard into any outrage upon the person of one who might have it in his power to retaliate so severely upon themselves. They continued obstinately at a stand, simply preventing his escape, when suddenly the tread of horses' feet arose upon the ear, and through a long vista were discovered a body of cavalry from the castle coming up at a charging pace to the main entrance of the college. Without pulling up on the outside, as hitherto they had always done, they expressed sufficiently the altered tone of the Landgrave's feelings towards the old chartered interests of Klosterheim, by plunging through the great archway of the college-gates; and then making way at the same furious pace through the assembled crowds, who broke rapidly away to the right and to the left, they reined up directly abreast of the city guard and their prisoners.

"Colonel Von Aremberg!" said St. Aldenheim, "I perceive your errand. To a soldier I surrender myself; to this tyrant of dungeons, who has betrayed more men, and cheated more gibbets of their due than ever he said *aves*, I will never lend an ear, though he should bear the orders of every Landgrave in Germany."

"You do well," replied the Colonel; "but for this man, Count, he bears no orders from any Landgrave, nor will ever again bear orders from the Landgrave of

X——. Gentlemen, you are all my prisoners; and you will accompany me to the castle. Count St. Aldenheim, I am sorry that there is no longer an exemption for yourself. Please to advance. If it will be any gratification to you, these men" (pointing to the city guard) "are prisoners also."

Here was a revolution of fortune that confounded everybody. The detested guardians of the city jail were themselves to tenant it; or, by a worse fate still, were to be consigned unpitied, and their case unjudged, to the dark and pestilent dungeons which lay below the Landgrave's castle. A few scattered cries of triumph were heard from the crowd; but they were drowned in a tumult of conflicting feelings. As human creatures, fallen under the displeasure of a despot with a judicial power of torture to enforce his investigations, even *they* claimed some compassion. But there arose, to call off attention from these less dignified objects of the public interest, a long train of gallant cavaliers, restored so capriciously to liberty, in order, as it seemed, to give the greater poignancy and bitterness to the instant renewal of their captivity. This was the very frenzy of despotism in its very moodiest state of excitement. Many began to think the Landgrave mad. If so, what a dreadful fate might be anticipated for the sons or representatives of so many noble families, gallant soldiers the greater part of them, with a nobleman of princely blood at their head, lying under the displeasure of a gloomy and infuriated tyrant, with unlimited means of executing the bloodiest suggestions of his vengeance. Then, in what way had the guardians of the jails come to be connected with any even imaginary offence? Supposing the Landgrave insane, his agents were not so; Colonel Von Aremberg was a man of shrewd and penetrating understanding; and this officer had clearly spoken in the tone of one, who, whilst announcing the sentence of another, sympathizes entirely with the justice and necessity of its harshness.

Something dropped from the miserable leader of the city guard, in his first confusion and attempt at self-defence, which rather increased than explained the mystery. "The Masque! the Masque!" This was the word which fell at intervals upon the ear of the listening crowd, as he sometimes directed his words in the way of apology and deprecation to Colonel Von Aremberg, who did not vouchsafe to listen, or of occasional explanation and discussion, as it was partially kept up between himself and one of his nearest partners in the imputed transgression. Two or three there might be seen in the crowd, whose looks avowed some nearer acquaintance with this mysterious allusion than it would have been safe to acknowledge. But, for the great body of spectators who accompanied the prisoners and their escort to the gates of the castle, it was pretty evident by their inquiring looks, and the fixed expression of wonder upon their features, that the whole affair, and its circumstances, were to them equally a subject of mystery for what was past, and of blind terror for what was to come.

CHAPTER IX.

The cavalcade, with its charge of prisoners, and its attendant train of spectators, halted at the gates of the *schloss*. This vast and antique pile had now come to be surveyed with dismal and revolting feelings, as the abode of a sanguinary despot. The dungeons and labyrinths of its tortuous passages, its gloomy halls of audience, with the vast corrridors which surmounted the innumerable flights of stairs — some noble, spacious, and in the Venetian taste, capable of admitting the march of an army — some spiral, steep, and so unusually narrow as to exclude two persons walking abreast; these, together with the numerous chapels erected in it to different saints by devotees, male or female, in the families of forgotten Landgraves through four centuries back; and finally the tribunals, or *gericht-kammern*, for dispensing justice, criminal or civil, to the city and territorial dependencies of Klosterheim; — all united to compose a body of impressive images, hallowed by great historical remembrances, or traditional stories, that from infancy to age dwelt upon the feelings of the Klosterheimers. Terror and superstitious dread predominated undoubtedly in the total impression; but the gentle virtues exhibited by a series of princes, who had made this their favorite residence, naturally enough terminated in mellowing the sternness of such associations into a religious awe, not without its own peculiar attractions. But at present, under the harsh and repulsive character of the reigning prince, everything took a new color from his ungenial habits. The superstitious legends, which had so immemorially peopled the *schloss* with spectral apparitions, now revived in its earliest strength. Never was Germany more dedicated to superstition in every shape than at this period. The wild tumultuous times, and the slight tenure upon which all men held their lives, naturally threw their thoughts much upon the other world; and communications with that, or its burthen of secrets, by every variety of agencies, ghosts, divination, natural magic, palmistry, or astrology, found in every city of the land more encouragement than ever.

It cannot, therefore, be surprising that the well-known apparition of the White Lady (a legend which affected Klosterheim through the fortunes of its Landgraves, no less than several other princely houses of Germany, descended from the same original stock), should about this time have been seen in the dusk of the evening at some of the upper windows in the castle, and once in a lofty gallery of the great chapel during the vesper service. This lady, generally known by the name of the White Lady Agnes, or *Lady Agnes of Weissemburg*, is supposed to have lived in the 13th or 14th century, and from that time, even to our own days, the current belief is, that on the eve of any great crisis of good or evil fortune impending over the three or four illustrious houses of Germany which trace their origin from her, she makes her appearance in some conspicuous apartment, great baronial hall or chapel, of their several palaces, sweeping along in white robes and a voluminous train. Her appearance of late in the *schloss* of Klosterheim, confidently believed by the great body of the people, was hailed with secret pleasure, as forerunning some great change in the Landgrave's family, — which was but another name for better days to themselves, whilst of necessity it menaced some great evil to the prince himself. Hope, therefore, was predominant in their prospects, and in the supernatural intimations of coming changes; — yet awe and deep religious feeling mingled with their hope. Of chastisement approaching to the Landgrave they felt assured, — some dim religious judgment like that which brooded over the house of Œdipus, was now at hand, — that was the universal impression. His gloomy asceticism of life seemed to argue secret crimes, — these were to be brought to light; — for these, and for his recent tyranny, prosperous as it had seemed for a moment, chastisements were now impending; and something of the awe which belonged to a prince so marked out for doom and fatal catastrophe, seemed to attach itself to his mansion, — more especially, as it was there only that the signs and portents of the coming woe had revealed themselves in the apparition of the White Lady.

Under this superstitious impression, many of the spectators paused at the entrance of the castle, and lingered in the portal, though presuming that the chamber of justice, according to the frank old usage of Germany, was still open to all comers. Of this notion they were speedily disabused by the sudden retreat of the few who had penetrated into the first antechamber. These persons were harshly repelled in a contumelious manner, and read to the astonished citizens another lesson upon the new arts of darkness and concealment, with which the Landgrave found it necessary to accompany his new acts of tyranny.

Von Aremberg and his prisoners, thus left alone in one of the antechambers, waited no long time before they were summoned to the presence of the Landgrave.

After pacing along a number of corridors, all carpeted so as to return no sound to their footsteps, they arrived in a little hall, from which a door suddenly opened, upon a noiseless signal exchanged with an usher outside, and displayed before them a long gallery, with a table and a few seats arranged at the further end. Two gentlemen were seated at the table, anxiously examining papers; in one of whom it was easy to recognize the wily glance of the Italian minister, the other was the Landgrave.

This prince was now on the verge of fifty, strikingly handsome in his features, and of imposing presence, from the union of a fine person with manners unusually dignified. No man understood better the art of restraining his least governable impulses of anger or malignity within the decorums of his rank. And even his worst passions, throwing a gloomy, rather than terrific air upon his features, served less to alarm and revolt, than to impress the sense of secret distrust. Of late indeed, from the too evident indications of the public hatred, his sallies of passion had become wilder and more ferocious, and his self-command less habitually conspicuous. But in general, a gravity of insiduous courtesy disguised from all but penetrating eyes the treacherous purpose of his heart.

The Landgrave bowed to the Count St. Aldenheim; and, pointing to a chair, begged him to understand that he wished to do nothing inconsistent with his regard for the Palsgrave his brother; and would be content with his parole of honor to pursue no further any conspiracy against himself, in which he might too thoughtlessly have engaged, and with his retirement from the city of Klosterheim.

The Count St Aldenheim replied, that he and all the

other cavaliers present, according to his belief, stood upon the same footing: that they had harbored no thought of conspiracy, unless that name could attach to a purpose of open expostulation with his Highness on the outraged privileges of their corporation as a university: that he wished not for any distinction of treatment in a case when all were equal offenders, or none at all: and finally, that he believed the sentence of exile from Klosterheim would be cheerfully accepted by all, or most of those present.

Adorni, the minister, shook his head, and glanced significantly at the Landgrave during this answer. The Landgrave coldly replied, that if he could suppose the Count to speak sincerely, it was evident that he was little aware to what length his companions, or some of them, had pushed their plots. "Here are the proofs!" and he pointed to the papers.

"And now, gentlemen," said he, turning to the students, "I marvel that you, being cavaliers of family, and doubtless holding yourselves men of honor, should beguile these poor knaves into certain ruin, whilst yourselves could reap nothing but a brief mockery of the authority which you could not hope to evade."

Thus called upon, the students and the city-guard told their tale, in which no contradictions could be detected. The city prison was not particularly well secured against attacks from without. To prevent, therefore, any sudden attempt at a rescue, the guard kept watch by turns. One man watched two hours, traversing the different passages of the prison; and was then relieved. At three o'clock on the preceding night, pacing a winding lobby, brightly illuminated, the man who kept that watch was suddenly met by a person wearing a masque, and armed at all points. His surprise and consternation were great, and the more so as the steps of The Masque were soundless, though the floor was a stone one. The guard, but slightly prepared to meet an attack, would, however, have resisted or raised an alarm; but The Masque instantly levelling a pistol at his head with one hand, with the other had thrown open the door of an empty cell, indicating to the man by signs that he must enter it. With this intimation he had necessarily complied; and The Masque had immediately turned the key upon him. Of what followed he knew nothing, until aroused by his comrades setting him at liberty, after some time had been wasted in searching for him.

The students had a pretty uniform tale to report. A Masque, armed cap-a-pie as described by the guard, had visited each of their cells in succession; had instructed them by signs to dress; and then, pointing to the door, by a series of directions all communicated in the same dumb show, had assembled them together, thrown open the prison door, and, pointing to their college, had motioned them thither. This motion they had seen no cause to disobey, presuming their dismissal to be according to the mode which best pleased his Highness ; and not ill-pleased at finding so peaceful a termination to a summons which at first, from its mysterious shape and the solemn hour of night, they had understood as tending to some more formidable issue.

It was observed that neither the Landgrave nor his minister treated this report of so strange a transaction with the scorn which had been anticipated. Both listened attentively, and made minute inquiries as to every circumstance of the dress and appointments of the mysterious Masque. What was his height? By what road, or in what direction had he disappeared? These questions answered, his Highness and his minister consulted a few minutes together; and then, turning to Von Aremberg, bade him for the present dismiss the prisoners to their homes, an act of grace which seemed likely to do him service at the present crisis; but at the same time to take sufficient security for their reappearance. This done, the whole body were liberated.

CHAPTER X.

All Klosterheim was confounded by the story of the mysterious Masque. For the story had been rapidly dispersed; and on the same day it was made known in another shape. A notice was affixed to the walls of several public places in these words:—

"Landgrave, beware! henceforth not you, but I, govern in Klosterheim.

(Signed) "The Masque."

And this was no empty threat. Very soon it became apparent that some mysterious agency was really at work to counteract the Landgrave's designs. Sentinels were carried off from solitary posts. Guards even of a dozen men were silently trepanned from their stations. By and by, other attacks were made, even more alarming, upon domestic security. Was there a burgomaster amongst the citizens, who had made himself conspicuously a tool of the Landgrave, or had opposed the Imperial interest? He was carried off in the night-time from his house, and probably from the city. At first this was an easy task. Nobody apprehending any special danger to himself, no special preparations were made to meet it. But, as it soon became apparent in what cause The Masque was moving, every person who knew himself obnoxious to attack, took means to face it. Guards were multiplied; arms were repaired in every house; alarm bells were hung. For a time the danger seemed to diminish. The attacks were no longer so frequent. Still, wherever they were attempted, they succeeded just as before. It seemed, in fact, that all the precautions taken had no other effect than to warn The Masque of his own danger, and to place him more vigilantly on his guard. Aware of new defences raising, it seemed that he waited to see the course they would take; once master of that, he was ready (as it appeared) to contend with them as successfully as before.

Nothing could exceed the consternation of the city. Those even, who did not fall within the apparent rule which governed the attacks of The Masque, felt a sense of indefinite terror hanging over them. Sleep was no longer safe; the seclusion of a man's private hearth, the secrecy of bedrooms, was no longer a protection. Locks gave way, bars fell, doors flew open, as if by magic, before him. Arms seemed useless. In some instances a party of as many as ten or a dozen persons had been removed without rousing disturbance in the neighborhood. Nor was this the only circumstance of mystery. Whither he could remove his victims, was even more incomprehensible than the means by which he succeeded. All was darkness and fear ; and the whole city was agitated with panic.

It began now to be suggested that a nightly guard should be established, having fixed stations or points of rendezvous, and at intervals parading the streets. This was cheerfully assented to ; for after the first week of the mysterious attacks, it began to be observed that the Imperial party were attacked indiscriminately with the Swedish. Many students publicly declared that they had been dogged through a street or two by an armed Masque ; others had been suddenly confronted by him in unfrequented parts of the city in the dead of night, and were on the point of being attacked, when some alarm, or the approach of distant footsteps, had caused him to disappear. The students, indeed, more particularly, seemed objects of attack ; and, as they were pretty generally attached to the Imperial interest, the motives of The Masque were no longer judged to be political. Hence it happened that the students came forward in a body, and volunteered as members of the nightly guard. Being young, military for the most part in their habits, and trained to support the hardships of night-watching, they seemed peculiarly fitted for the service ; and, as the case was no longer of a nature to awaken the suspicions of the Landgrave, they were generally accepted and enrolled; and with the more readiness, as the known friends of that prince came forward at the same time.

A night-watch was thus established, which promised security to the city, and a respite from their mysterious alarms. It was distributed into eight or ten divisions, posted at different points, whilst a central one traversed the whole city at stated periods, and overlooked the local stations. Such an arrangement was wholly unknown at that time in every part of Germany, and was hailed with general applause.

To the astonishment, however, of everybody, it proved wholly ineffectual. Houses were entered as before; the college chambers proved no sanctuary; indeed, they were attacked with a peculiar obstinacy, which was understood to express a spirit of retaliation for the alacrity of the students in combining for the public protection. People were carried off as before. And continual notices affixed to the gates of the college, the convents, or the *schloss*, with the signature of *The Masque*, announced to the public his determination to persist, and his contempt of the measures organized against him.

The alarm of the citizens now became greater than ever. The danger was one which courage could not face, nor prudence make provision for, nor wiliness evade. All alike, who had once been marked out for attack, sooner or later fell victims to the obstinacy of this mysterious foe. To have received even an individual warning, availed them not at all. Sometimes it happened, that, having received notice of suspicious circumstances indicating that The Masque had turned his attention upon themselves, they would assemble round their dwellings, or in their very chambers, a band of armed men sufficient to set the danger at defiance. But no sooner had they relaxed in these costly and troublesome arrangements, no sooner was the sense of peril lulled, and an opening made for their unrelenting enemy, than he glided in with his customary success; and in a morning or two after, it was announced to the city that they also were numbered with his victims.

Even yet it seemed that something remained in reserve to augment the terrors of the citizens, and push them to excess. Hitherto there had been no reason to think that any murderous violence had occurred in the mysterious rencontres between The Masque and his victims. But of late, in those houses, or college chambers, from which the occupiers had disappeared, traces of bloodshed were apparent in some instances, and of ferocious conflict in others. Sometimes a profusion of hair was scattered on the ground; sometimes fragments of dress, or splinters of weapons. Everything marked that on both sides, as this mysterious agency advanced, the passions increased in intensity; determination and murderous malignity on the one side, and the fury of resistance on the other.

At length the last consummation was given to the public panic; for, as if expressly to put an end to all doubts upon the spirit in which he conducted his warfare, in one house where the bloodshed had been so great as to argue some considerable loss of life, a notice was left behind in the following terms: "Thus it is that I punish resistance; mercy to a cheerful submission; but henceforth death to the obstinate! — The Masque."

What was to be done? Some counselled a public deprecation of his wrath, addressed to The Masque. But this, had it even offered any chance of succeeding, seemed too abject an act of abasement to become a large city. Under any circumstances, it was too humiliating a confession, that, in a struggle with one man (for no more had avowedly appeared upon the scene), they were left defeated and at his mercy. A second party counselled a treaty; would it not be possible to learn the ultimate objects of The Masque? and, if such as seemed capable of being entertained with honor, to concede to him his demands, in exchange for security to the city, and immunity from future molestation? It was true that no man knew where to seek him: personally he was hidden from their reach; but everybody knew how to find him: he was amongst them; in their very centre; and whatever they might address to him in a public notice, would be sure of speedily reaching his eye.

After some deliberation, a summons was addressed to The Masque, and exposed on the college gates, demanding of him a declaration of his purposes, and the price which he expected for suspending them. The next day an answer appeared in the same situation, avowing the intention of The Masque to come forward with ample explanation of his motives at a proper crisis, till which "more blood must flow in Klosterheim."

CHAPTER XI.

MEANTIME the Landgrave was himself perplexed and alarmed. Hitherto he had believed himself possessed of all the intrigues, plots or conspiracies, which threatened his influence in the city. Among the students and among the citizens he had many spies, who communicated to him whatsoever they could learn, which was sometimes more than the truth, and sometimes a good deal less. But now he was met by a terrific antagonist, who moved in darkness, careless of his power, inaccessible to his threats, and apparently as reckless as himself of the quality of his means.

Adorni, with all his Venetian subtlety, was now as much at fault as everybody else. In vain had they deliberated together, day after day, upon his probable purposes; in vain had they schemed to intercept his person, or offered high rewards for tracing his retreats. Snares had been laid for him in vain; every wile had proved abortive, every plot had been counterplotted. And both involuntarily confessed that they had now met with their master.

Vexed and confounded, fears for the future struggling with mortification for the past, the Landgrave was sitting, late at night, in the long gallery where he usually held his councils. He was reflecting with anxiety on the peculiarly unpropitious moment at which his new enemy had come upon the stage — the very crisis of the struggle between the Swedish and Imperial interest in Klosterheim, which would ultimately determine his own place and value in the estimate of his new allies. He was not of a character to be easily duped by mystery. Yet he could not but acknowledge to himself that there was something calculated to impress awe, and the sort of fear which is connected with the supernatural, in the sudden appearances, and vanishings as sudden, of The Masque. He came no one could guess whence, retreated no one could guess whither; was intercepted, and yet eluded arrest; and if half the stories in circulation could be credited, seemed inaudible in his steps, at pleasure to make himself invisible and impalpable to the very hands stretched out to detain him. Much of this, no doubt, was wilful exaggeration, or the fictions of fears self-deluded. But enough remained, after every allowance, to justify an extraordinary interest in so singular a being; and the Landgrave could not avoid wishing that chance might offer an opportunity to himself of observing him.

Profound silence had for some time reigned throughout the castle. A clock which stood in the room, broke it for a moment by striking the quarters; and, raising his eyes, the Landgrave perceived that it was past two. He rose to retire for the night, and stood for a moment musing with one hand resting upon the table. A momentary feeling of awe came across him, as his eyes travelled through the gloom at the lower end of the room, on the sudden thought that a being so mysterious, and capable of piercing through so many impediments to the interior of every mansion in Klosterheim, was doubtless likely enough to visit the castle; nay, it would be no ways improbable that he should penetrate to this very room. What bars had yet been found sufficient to repel him? And who could pretend to calculate the hour of his visit? This night even might be the time which he would select. Thinking thus, the Landgrave was suddenly aware of a dusky figure entering the room by a door at the lower end. The room had the length and general proportions of a gallery, and the further end was so remote from the candles which stood on the Landgrave's table, that the deep gloom was but slightly penetrated by their rays. Light, however, there was, sufficient to display the outline of a figure slowly and inaudibly advancing up the room. It could not be said that the figure advanced stealthily; on the contrary, its motion, carriage, and bearing, were in the highest degree dignified and solemn. But the feeling of a stealthy purpose was suggested by the perfect silence of its tread. The motion of a shadow could not be more noiseless. And this circumstance confirmed the Landgrave's first impression, that now he was on the point of accomplishing his recent wish, and meeting that mysterious being who was the object of so much awe, and the author of so far-spread a panic.

He was right; it was indeed The Masque, armed cap-a-pie as usual. He advanced with an equable and determined step in the direction of the Landgrave. Whether he saw his Highness, who stood a little in the shade of a large cabinet, could not be known; the Landgrave doubted not that he did. He was a prince of firm nerves by constitution, and of great intrepidity, — yet, as one who shared in the superstitions of his age, he could not be expected entirely to suppress an emotion of indefinite apprehension as he now beheld the solemn approach of a being, who, by some unaccountable means, had trepanned so many different individuals from so many different houses, most of them prepared for self-defence, and fenced in by the protection of stone walls, locks, and bars.

The Landgrave, however, lost none of his presence of mind; and in the midst of his discomposure, as his eye fell upon the habiliments of this mysterious person, and the arms and military accoutrements which he bore, naturally his thoughts settled upon the more earthly means of annoyance which this martial apparition carried about him. The Landgrave was himself unarmed, — he had no arms even within reach, — nor was it possible for him in his present situation very speedily to summon assistance. With these thoughts passing rapidly through his mind, and sensible that, in any view of his nature and powers, the being now in his presence was a very formidable antagonist, the Landgrave could not but feel relieved from a burden of anxious tremors, when he saw The Masque suddenly turn towards a door which opened about half way up the room, and lead into a picture-gallery at right angles with the room in which they both were.

Into the picture-gallery The Masque passed at the same solemn pace, without apparently looking at the Landgrave. This movement seemed to argue, either that he purposely declined an interview with the Prince, and *that* might argue fear, or that he had not been aware of his presence; — either supposition, as implying something of human infirmity, seemed incompatible with supernatural faculties. Partly upon this consideration, and partly perhaps because he suddenly recollected that the road taken by The Masque would lead him directly past the apartments of the old seneschal, where assistance might be summoned, the Landgrave found his spirits at this moment revive. The consciousness of rank and birth also came to his aid, and that sort of disdain of the aggressor, which possesses every man — brave or cowardly alike —

within the walls of his own dwelling: — unarmed as he was, he determined to pursue, and perhaps to speak.

The restraints of high breeding, and the ceremonious decorum of his rank, involuntarily checked the Landgrave from pursuing with a hurried pace. He advanced with his habitual gravity of step, so that The Masque was half way down the gallery before the Prince entered it. This gallery, furnished on each side with pictures, of which some were portraits, was of great length. The Masque and the Prince continued to advance, preserving a pretty equal distance. It did not appear by any sign or gesture that The Masque was aware of the Landgrave's pursuit. Suddenly, however, he paused — drew his sword — halted; the Landgrave also halted; then turning half round, and waving with his hand to the Prince so as to solicit his attention, slowly The Masque elevated the point of his sword to the level of a picture — it was the portrait of a young cavalier in a hunting dress, blooming with youth and youthful energy. The Landgrave turned pale, trembled, and was ruefully agitated. The Masque kept his sword in its position for half a minute; then dropping it, shook his head, and raised his hand with a peculiar solemnity of expression. The Landgrave recovered himself — his features swelled with passion — he quickened his step, and again followed in pursuit.

The Masque, however, had by this time turned out of the gallery into a passage, which, after a single curve, terminated in the private room of the seneschal. Believing that his ignorance of the localities was thus leading him on to certain capture, the Landgrave pursued more leisurely. The passage was dimly lighted; every image floated in a cloudy obscurity; and, upon reaching the curve, it seemed to the Landgrave that The Masque was just on the point of entering the seneschal's room. No other door was heard to open; and he felt assured that he had seen the lofty figure of The Masque gliding into that apartment. He again quickened his steps; a light burned within, the door stood ajar; quietly the Prince pushed it open, and entered with the fullest assurance that he should here at length overtake the object of his pursuit.

Great was his consternation upon finding in a room, which presented no outlet, not a living creature except the elderly seneschal, who lay quietly sleeping in his arm-chair. The first impulse of the Prince was to awaken him roughly, that he might summon aid and co-operate in the search. One glance at a paper upon the table arrested his hand. He saw a name written there, interesting to his fears beyond all others in the world. His eye was riveted as by fascination to the paper. He read one instant. That satisfied him that the old seneschal must be overcome by no counterfeit slumbers, when he could thus surrender a secret of capital importance to the gaze of that eye from which above all others he must desire to screen it. One moment he deliberated with himself; the old man stirred, and muttered in his dreams; the Landgrave seized the paper and stood irresolute for an instant whether to await his wakening, and authoritatively to claim what so nearly concerned his own interest, or to retreat with it from the room before the old man should be aware of the Prince's visit, or his own loss.

But the seneschal, wearied perhaps with some unusual exertion, had but moved in his chair; again he composed himself to deep slumber, made deeper by the warmth of a hot fire. The raving of the wind, as it whistled round this angle of the *schloss*, drowned all sounds that could have disturbed him. The Landgrave secreted the paper; nor did any sense of his rank and character interpose to check him in an act so unworthy of an honorable cavalier. Whatever crimes he had hitherto committed or authorized, this was perhaps the first instance in which he had offended by an instance of petty knavery. He retired with the stealthy pace of a robber anxious to evade detection; and stole back to his own apartments with an overpowering interest in the discovery he had made so accidentally, and with an anxiety to investigate it farther, which absorbed for the time all other cares, and banished from his thoughts even The Masque himself, whose sudden appearance and retreat had in fact thrown into his hands the secret which now so exclusively disturbed him.

CHAPTER XII.

MEANTIME The Masque continued to harass the Landgrave, to baffle many of his wiles, and to neutralize his most politic schemes. In one of the many placards which he affixed to the castle gates, he described the Landgrave as ruling in Klosterheim by day, and himself by night. Sarcasms such as these, together with the practical insults which The Masque continually offered to the Landgrave, by foiling his avowed designs, embittered the Prince's existence. The injury done to his political schemes of ambition at this particular crisis was irreparable. One after one, all the agents and tools by whom he could hope to work upon the counsels of the Klosterheim authorities, had been removed. Losing *their* influence, he had lost every prop of his own. Nor was this all; he was reproached by the general voice of the city as the original cause of a calamity, which he had since shown himself impotent to redress. He it was, and his cause, which had drawn upon the people, so fatally trepanned, the hostility of the mysterious Masque. But for his Highness, all the burgomasters, captains, city-officers,

&c., would now be sleeping in their beds; whereas the best fate which could be surmised for the most of them, was, that they were sleeping in dungeons; some perhaps in their graves. And thus the Landgrave's cause not merely lost its most efficient partisans, but through their loss determined the wavering against him, alienated the few who remained of his own faction, and gave strength and encouragement to the general disaffection which had so long prevailed.

Thus it happened that the conspirators, or suspected conspirators, could not be brought to trial, or to punishment without a trial. Any spark of fresh irritation falling upon the present combustible temper of the populace, would not fail to produce an explosion. Fresh conspirators, and real ones, were thus encouraged to arise. The university, the city, teemed with plots. The government of the Prince was exhausted with the growing labor of tracing and counteracting them. And, by little and little, matters came into such a condition, that the control of the city, though still continuing in the Landgrave's hands, was maintained by mere martial force, and at the very point of the sword. And in no long time, it was feared, that with so general a principle of hatred to combine the populace, and so large a body of military students to head them, the balance of power, already approaching to an equipoise, would be turned against the Landgrave's government. And, in the best event, his Highness could now look for nothing from their love. All might be reckoned for lost that could not be extorted by force.

This state of things had been brought about by the dreadful Masque, seconded, no doubt, by those whom he had emboldened and aroused within; and, as the climax and crowning injury of the whole, every day unfolded more and more the vast importance which Klosterheim would soon possess as the centre and key of the movements to be anticipated in the coming campaign. An electoral cap would perhaps reward the services of the Landgrave in the general pacification, if he could present himself at the German Diet as the possessor *de facto* of Klosterheim and her territorial dependencies, and with some imperfect possession *de jure;* still more, if he could plead the merit of having brought over this state, so important from local situation, as a willing ally to the Swedish interest. But to this, a free vote of the city was an essential preliminary; and from that, through the machinations of The Masque, he was now further than ever.

The temper of the Prince began to give way under these accumulated provocations. An enemy forever aiming his blows with the deadliest effect; forever stabbing in the dark; yet charmed and consecrated from all retaliation; always met with, never to be found! The Landgrave ground his teeth, clenched his fists, with spasms of fury. He quarrelled with his ministers; swore at the officers; cursed the sentinels; and the story went through Klosterheim that he had kicked Adorni.

Certain it was, under whatever stimulus, that Adorni put forth much more zeal at last for the apprehension of The Masque. Come what would, he publicly avowed that six days more should not elapse without the arrest of this "ruler of Klosterheim by night." He had a scheme for the purpose, a plot baited for snaring him; and he pledged his reputation as a minister and an intriguer, upon its entire success.

On the following day, invitations were issued by Adorni, in his Highness's name, to a masqued ball on that day week. The fashion of masqued entertainments had been recently introduced from Italy into this sequestered nook of Germany; and here, as there, it had been abused to purposes of criminal intrigue.

Spite of the extreme unpopularity of the Landgrave with the low and middle classes of the city, among the highest his little court still continued to furnish a central resort to the rank and high blood, converged in such unusual proportion within the walls of Klosterheim. The *schloss* was still looked to as the standard and final court of appeal in all matters of taste, elegance, and high breeding. Hence it naturally happened that everybody, with any claims to such an honor, was anxious to receive a ticket of admission; — it became the test for ascertaining a person's pretensions to mix in the first circles of society ; and with this extraordinary zeal for obtaining an admission, naturally increased the minister's rigor and fastidiousness in pressing the usual investigation of the claimant's qualifications. Much offence was given on both sides, and many sneers hazarded at the minister himself, whose pretensions were supposed to be of the lowest description. But the result was, that exactly twelve hundred cards were issued ; these were regularly numbered, and below the device engraved upon the card was impressed a seal bearing the arms and motto of the Landgraves of X——.

Every precaution was taken for carrying into effect the scheme, with all its details, as concerted by Adorni ; and the third day of the following week was announced as the day of the expected *fête*.

CHAPTER XIII.

The morning of the important day at length arrived, and all Klosterheim was filled with expectation — even those who were not amongst the invited shared in the anxiety; for a great scene was looked for, and perhaps some tragical explosion. The undertaking of Adorni was known; it had been published abroad that he was solemnly pledged to effect the arrest of The Masque; and by many it was believed that he would so far succeed, at the least, as to bring on a public collision with that extraordinary personage. As to the issue, most people were doubtful; The Masque having hitherto so uniformly defeated the best-laid schemes for his apprehension. But it was hardly questioned that the public challenge offered to him by Adorni would succeed in bringing him before the public eye. This challenge had taken the shape of a public notice posted up in the places where The Masque had usually affixed his own; and it was to the following effect: — "That the noble strangers now in Klosterheim, and others invited to the Landgrave's *fête*, who might otherwise feel anxiety in presenting themselves at the *schloss,* from an apprehension of meeting with the criminal disturber of the public peace, known by the appellation of The Masque, were requested by authority to lay aside all apprehensions of that nature, as the most energetic measures had been adopted to prevent or chastise upon the spot any such insufferable intrusion; and for The Masque himself, if he presumed to disturb the company by his presence, he would be seized where he stood, and without further inquiry committed to the Provost Marshal for instant execution; — on which account, all persons were warned carefully to forbear from intrusions of simple curiosity, since in the hurry of the moment it might be difficult to make the requisite distinctions."

It was anticipated that this insulting notice would not long go without an answer from The Masque. Accordingly, on the following morning, a placard, equally conspicuous, was posted up in the same public places, side by side with that to which it replied. It was couched in the following terms: — "That he who ruled by night in Klosterheim, could not suppose himself to be excluded from a nocturnal *fête* given by any person in that city; that he must be allowed to believe himself invited by the Prince, and would certainly have the honor to accept his Highness's obliging summons. With regard to the low personalities addressed to himself, that he could not descend to notice anything of that nature coming from a man so abject as Adorni, until he should first have cleared himself from the imputation of having been a tailor in Venice at the time of the Spanish conspiracy in 1618, and banished from that city, not for any suspicions that could have settled upon him and his eight journeymen as making up one conspirator, but on account of some professional tricks in making a doublet for the Doge. For the rest, he repeated that he would not fail to meet the Landgrave and his honorable company."

All Klosterheim laughed at this public mortification offered to Adorni's pride; for that minister had incurred the public dislike as a foreigner, and their hatred on the score of private character. Adorni himself foamed at the mouth with rage, impotent for the present, but which he prepared to give deadly effect to at the proper time. But whilst it laughed, Klosterheim also trembled. Some persons, indeed, were of opinion, that the answer of The Masque was a mere sportive effusion of malice or pleasantry from the students, who had suffered so much by his annoyances. But the majority, amongst whom was Adorni himself, thought otherwise. Apart, even from the reply, or the insult which had provoked it, the general impression was, that The Masque would not have failed in attending a festival which, by the very costume which it imposed, offered so favorable a cloak to his own mysterious purposes. In this persuasion, Adorni took all the precautions which personal vengeance and Venetian subtlety could suggest, for availing himself of the single opportunity that would perhaps ever be allowed him for entrapping this public enemy, who had now become a private one to himself.

These various incidents had furnished abundant matter for conversation in Klosterheim, and had carried the public expectation to the highest pitch of anxiety, some time before the great evening arrived. Leisure had been allowed for fear, and every possible anticipation of the wildest character, to unfold themselves. Hope, even, amongst many, was a predominant sensation. Ladies were preparing for hysterics. Cavaliers, besides the swords which they wore as regular articles of dress, were providing themselves with stilettoes against any sudden rencontre hand to hand, or any unexpected surprise. Armorers and furbishers of weapons were as much in request as the more appropriate artists who minister to such festal occasions. These again were summoned to give their professional aid and attendance to an extent so much out of proportion to their numbers and their natural powers of exertion, that they were harassed beyond all physical capacity of endurance, and found their ingenuity more heavily taxed to find personal substitutes amongst the trades most closely connected with their own, than in any of the contrivances which more properly fell within the business of their own art. Tailors, horse-milliners, shoemakers, friseurs, drapers, mercers, tradesmen of every description, and servants of every class and denomination were summoned to a sleepless activity — each in his several vocation, or in some which he undertook by proxy. Artificers who had escaped on political motives from Nuremburg and other Imperial cities, or from the sack of Magdeburg, now showed their ingenuity, and their readiness to earn the bread of industry; and if Klosterheim resembled a hive in the close-packed condition of its inhabitants, it was now seen that the resemblance held good hardly less in the industry which, upon a sufficient excitement, it was able to develope. But in the midst of all this stir, din, and unprecedented activity, whatever occupation each man found for his thoughts or for his hands in his separate employments, all hearts were mastered by one domineering interest — the approaching collision of the Landgrave, before his assembled court, with the mysterious agent who had so long troubled his repose.

CHAPTER XIV.

The day at length arrived; the guards were posted in unusual strength; the pages of honor, and servants in their state-dresses, were drawn up in long and gorgeous files along the sides of the vast gothic halls, which ran in continued succession from the front of the *schloss* to the more modern saloons in the rear; bands of military music, collected from amongst the foreign prisoners of various nations at Vienna, were stationed in their national costume — Italian, Hungarian, Turkish, or Croatian — in the lofty galleries or corridors which ran round the halls; and the deep thunders of the kettle-drums, relieved by cymbals and wind-instruments, began to fill the mazes of the palace as early as seven o'clock in the evening; for at that hour, according to the custom then established in Germany, such entertainments commenced. Repeated volleys from long lines of musketeers, drawn up in the square, and at the other entrances of the palace, with the deep roar of artillery, announced the arrival of the more distinguished visitors; amongst whom it was rumored that several officers in supreme command from the Swedish camp, already collected in the neighborhood, were this night coming *incognito* — availing themselves of their masques to visit the Landgrave, and improve the terms of their alliance, whilst they declined the risk which they might have brought on themselves by too open a visit in their own avowed characters and persons, to a town so unsettled in its state of feeling, and so friendly to the Emperor, as Klosterheim had notoriously become.

From seven to nine o'clock, in one unbroken line of succession, gorgeous parties streamed along through the halls, a distance of full half a quarter of a mile, until they were checked by the barriers erected at the entrance to the first of the entertaining rooms, as the station for examining the tickets of admission. This duty was fulfilled in a way which, though really rigorous in the extreme, gave no inhospitable annoyance to the visitors — the barriers themselves concealed their jealous purpose of hostility, and in a manner disavowed the secret awe and mysterious terror which brooded over the evening, by the beauty of their external appearance. They presented a triple line of gilt lattice-work, rising to a great altitude, and connected with the fretted roof by pendent draperies of the most magnificent velvet, intermingled with banners and heraldic trophies suspended from the ceiling, and at intervals slowly agitated in the currents which now and then swept these aerial heights. In the centre of the lattice opened a single gate, on each side of which was stationed a couple of sentinels armed to the teeth; and this arrangement was repeated three times, so rigorous was the vigilance employed. At the second of the gates, where the bearer of a forged ticket would have found himself in a sort of trap, with absolutely no possibility of escape, every individual of each successive party presented his card of admission, and, fortunately for the convenience of the company, in consequence of the particular precaution used, one moment's inspection sufficed. The cards had been issued to the parties invited not very long before the time of assembling; consequently, as each was sealed with a private seal of the Landgrave's sculptured elaborately with his armorial bearings, forgery would have been next to impossible.

These arrangements, however, were made rather to relieve the company from the too powerful terrors which haunted them, and to possess them from the first with a sense of security, than for the satisfaction of the Landgrave or his minister. They were sensible that The Masque had it in his power to command an access from the interior — and this it seemed next to impossible altogether to prevent; nor was *that* indeed the wish of Adorni, but rather to facilitate his admission, and afterwards, when satisfied of his actual presence, to bar up all possibility of retreat. Accordingly, the interior arrangements, though perfectly prepared, and ready to close up at the word of command, were for the present but negligently enforced.

Thus stood matters at nine o'clock, by which time upwards of a thousand persons had assembled; and in ten minutes more an officer reported that the whole twelve hundred were present without one defaulter.

The Landgrave had not yet appeared, his minister having received the company; nor was he expected to appear for an hour — in reality, he was occupied in political discussion with some of the illustrious *incognitos.* But this did not interfere with the progress of the festival; and at this moment nothing could be more impressive than the far-stretching splendors of the spectacle.

In one immense saloon, twelve hundred cavaliers and ladies, attired in the unrivalled pomp of that age, were arranging themselves for one of the magnificent Hungarian dances, which the Emperor's court at Vienna had transplanted to the camp of Wallenstein, and thence to all the great houses of Germany. Bevies of noble women, in every variety of fanciful costume, but in each considerable group presenting deep masses of black or purple velvet, on which, with the most striking advantage of radiant relief, lay the costly pearl ornaments, or the sumptuous jewels so generally significant in those times of high ancestral pretensions, intermingled with the drooping plumes of martial cavaliers, who presented almost universally the soldierly air of frankness which belongs to active service, mixed with the Castilian *grandezza* that still breathed through the camps of Germany, emanating originally from the magnificent courts of Brussels, of Madrid, and of Vienna, and propagated to this age by the links of Tilly, the Bavarian commander, and Wallenstein, the more than princely commander for the Emperor. Figures and habiliments so commanding were of themselves enough to fill the eye and occupy the imagination ; but, beyond all this, feelings of awe and mystery, under more shapes than one, brooded over the whole scene, and diffused a tone of suspense and intense excitement throughout the vast assembly. It was known that illustrious strangers were present *incognito*. There now began to be some reason for anticipating a great battle in the neighborhood. The men were now present perhaps, the very hands were now visibly displayed for the coming dance, which in a few days or even hours (so rapid were the movements at this period) were to wield the truncheon that might lay the Catholic empire prostrate, or might mould the destiny of Europe for centuries. Even this feeling gave way to one still more enveloped in shades — The Masque ! Would he keep his promise and appear ? might he not even now be moving amongst them ? may he not, even at this very moment, thought each person, secretly be near me — or even touching myself — or haunting my own steps?

Yet again, thought most people (for at that time hardly anybody affected to be incredulous in matters allied to the supernatural), was this mysterious being liable to touch? Was he not of some impassive nature, inaudible, invisible, impalpable? Many of his escapes, if truly reported, seemed to argue as much. If, then, connected with the spiritual world, was it with the good or the evil in that inscrutable region? But then the bloodshed, the torn dresses, the marks of deadly struggle, which remained behind in some of those cases where mysterious disappearances had occurred, — these seemed undeniable arguments of murder, foul and treacherous murder. Every attempt, in short, to penetrate the mystery of this being's nature proved as abortive as the attempts to intercept his person; and all efforts at applying a solution to the difficulties of the case, made the mystery even more mysterious.

These thoughts, however, generally as they pervaded the company, would have given way for a time at least to the excitement of the scene; for a sudden clapping of hands from some officers of the household, to enforce attention, and as a signal to the orchestra in one of the galleries, at this moment proclaimed that the dances were on the point of commencing in another half minute, when suddenly a shriek from a female, and then a loud tumultuous cry from a multitude of voices, announced some fearful catastrophe; and in the next moment a shout of "Murder!" froze the blood of the timid amongst the company.

CHAPTER XV.

So vast was the saloon, that it had been impossible, through the maze of figures, the confusion of colors, and the mingling of a thousand voices, that anything should be perceived distinctly at the lower end of all that was now passing at the upper. Still, so awful is the mystery of life, and so hideous and accursed in man's imagination is every secret extinction of that consecrated lamp, that no news thrills so deeply, or travels so rapidly. Hardly could it be seen in what direction, or through whose communication, yet in less than a minute a movement of sympathizing horror, and uplifted hands, announced that the dreadful news had reached them. A murder, it was said, had been committed in the palace. Ladies began to faint; others hastened away in search of friends; others to learn the news more accurately; and some of the gentlemen, who thought themselves sufficiently privileged by rank, hurried off with a stream of agitated inquirers to the interior of the castle, in search of the scene itself. A few only passed the guard in the first moments of confusion, and penetrated with the agitated Adorni through the long and winding passages, into the very scene of the murder. A rumor had prevailed for a moment that the Landgrave was himself the victim; and as the road by which the agitated household conducted them took a direction towards his Highness's suite of rooms, at first Adorni had feared that result. Recovering his self-possession, however, at length, he learned that it was the poor old seneschal upon whom the blow had fallen. And he pressed on with more coolness to the dreadful spectacle.

The poor old man was stretched at his length on the floor. It did not seem that he had struggled with the murderer. Indeed, from some appearances, it seemed probable that he had been attacked whilst sleeping; and though he had received three wounds, it was pronounced by a surgeon that one of them (and *that*, from circumstances, the first) had been sufficient to extinguish life. He was discovered by his daughter, a woman who held some respectable place amongst the servants of the castle; and every presumption concurred in fixing the time of the dreadful scene to about one hour before.

"Such, gentlemen, are the acts of this atrocious monster, this Masque, who has so long been the scourge of Klosterheim," said Adorni to the strangers who had accompanied him, as they turned away on their return to the company; "but this very night, I trust, will put a bridle in his mouth."

"God grant it may be so!" said some. But others thought the whole case too mysterious for conjectures, and too solemn to be decided by presumptions. And in the midst of agitated discussions on the scene they had just witnessed, as well as the whole history of The Masque, the party returned to the saloon.

Under ordinary circumstances, this dreadful event would have damped the spirits of the company; as it was, it did but deepen the gloomy excitement which already had possession of all present, and raise a more intense expectation of the visit so publicly announced by The Masque. It seemed as though he had perpetrated this recent murder merely by way of reviving the impression of his own dreadful character in Klosterheim, which might have decayed a little of late, in all its original strength and freshness of novelty; or, as though he wished to send immediately before him an act of atrocity that should form an appropriate herald or harbinger of his own entrance upon the scene.

Dreadful, however, as this deed of darkness was, it seemed of too domestic a nature to exercise any continued influence upon so distinguished an assembly, so numerous, so splendid, and brought together at so distinguished a summons. Again, therefore, the masques prepared to mingle in the dance; again the signal was given; again the obedient orchestra preluded to the coming strains. In a moment more, the full tide of harmony swept along. The vast saloon, and its echoing roof, rang with the storm of music. The masques, with their floating plumes and jewelled caps, glided through the fine mazes of the Hungarian dances. All was one magnificent and tempestuous confusion, overflowing with the luxury of sound and sight, when suddenly, about midnight, a trumpet sounded, the Landgrave entered, and all was hushed. The glittering crowd arranged themselves in a half circle at the upper end of the room; his Highness went rapidly round saluting the company, and receiving their homage in return. A signal was again made; the music and the dancing were resumed; and such was the animation and the turbulent delight amongst the gayer part of the company, from the commingling of youthful blood with wine, lights, music, and festal conversation, that, with many, all thoughts of the dreadful Masque, who "reigned by night in Klosterheim," had faded before the exhilaration of the moment. Midnight had come; the dreadful apparition had not yet entered: young ladies began timidly to jest upon the subject, though as yet but faintly, and in a tone somewhat serious for a jest; and young cavaliers, who, to do them justice, had derived most part of their terrors from the superstitious view of the case, protested to their partners that if The Masque, on making his appearance, should conduct himself in a manner unbecoming a cavalier, or offensive to the ladies present, they should feel it their duty to chastise him; "though," said they, "with respect to old Adorni, should The Masque think proper to teach him better manners, or even to cane him, we shall not find it necessary to interfere."

Several of the *very* young ladies protested that, of all things, they should like to see a battle between old Adorni and The Masque, "such a love of a quiz that old Adorni is!" whilst others debated whether The Masque would turn out a young man or an old one; and a few elderly maidens mooted the point whether he were likely to be a "single" gentleman, or burdened with a "wife and family." These and similar discussions were increasing in vivacity, and kindling more and more gayety of repartee, when suddenly, with the effect of a funeral knell upon their mirth, a whisper began to circulate, that *there was one Masque too many in company.* Persons had been stationed by Adorni in different galleries, with instructions to note accurately the dress of every person in the company; to watch the motions of every one who gave the slightest cause for suspicion, by standing aloof from the rest of the assembly, or by any other peculiarity of manner; but, above all, to count the numbers of the total assembly. This last injunction was more easily obeyed than at first sight seemed possible. At this time, the Hungarian dances, which required a certain number of partners to execute the movements of the figure, were of themselves a sufficient register of the precise amount of persons engaged in them. And, as these dances continued for a long time undisturbed, this calculation once made, left no further computation necessary, than simply to take the account of all who stood otherwise engaged. This list being much the smaller one, was soon made; and the reports of several different observers, stationed in different galleries, and checked by each other, all tallied in reporting a total of just *twelve hundred and one persons*, after every allowance was made for the known members of the Landgrave's suite, who were all unmasqued.

This report was announced with considerable trepidation, in a very audible whisper to Adorni and the Landgrave. The buzz of agitation attracted instant attention; the whisper was loud enough to catch the ears of several; the news went rapidly kindling through the room that the company was too many by one: all the ladies trembled, their knees shook, their voices failed, they stopped in the very middle of questions, answers halted for their conclusion, and were never more remembered by either party; the very music began to falter, the lights seemed to wane and sicken; for the fact was now too evident — that The Masque had kept his appointment, and was at this moment in the room, "to meet the Landgrave and his honorable company."

Adorni and the Landgrave now walked apart from

the rest of the household, and were obviously consulting together on the next step to be taken, or on the proper moment for executing one which had already been decided on. Some crisis seemed approaching, and the knees of many ladies knocked together, as they anticipated some cruel or bloody act of vengeance. "Oh, poor Masque!" sighed a young lady in her tender-hearted concern for one who seemed now at the mercy of his enemies; "Do you think, sir," addressing her partner, "they will cut him to pieces?" —"Oh, that wicked old Adorni!" exclaimed another; "I know he will stick the poor Masque on one side, and somebody else will stick him on the other; I know he will, because the Masque called him a tailor: do you think he *was* a tailor, sir?" — "Why, really, madam, he walks like a tailor; but then he must be a very bad one, considering how ill his own clothes are made; and *that*, you know, is next door to being none at all. But see, his Highness is going to stop the music."

In fact, at that moment the Landgrave made a signal to the orchestra; the music ceased abruptly; and his Highness advancing to the company, who stood eagerly awaiting his words, said — "Illustrious and noble friends! for a very urgent and special cause I will request of you all to take your seats."

The company obeyed, every one sought the chair

next to him, or if a lady, accepted that which was offered by the cavalier at her side. The standers continually diminished. Two hundred were left, one hundred and fifty, eighty, sixty, twenty, till at last they were reduced to two, — both gentlemen, who had been attending upon ladies. They were suddenly aware of their own situation. One chair only remained out of twelve hundred. Eager to exonerate himself from suspicion, each sprang furiously to this seat; each attained it at the same moment, and each possessed himself of part at the same instant. As they happened to be two elderly corpulent men, the younger cavaliers, under all the restraints of the moment, the panic of the company, and the Landgrave's presence, could not forbear laughing; and the more spirited amongst the young ladies caught the infection.

His Highness was little in a temper to brook this levity; and hastened to relieve the joint occupants of the chair from the ridicule of their situation. "Enough!" he exclaimed, "enough! all my friends are requested to resume the situation most agreeable to them; my purpose is answered." — The prince was himself standing with all his household, and, as a point of respect, all the company rose. ("*As you were*," whispered the young soldiers to their fair companions.)

Adorni now came forward. "It is known," said he

"by trials more than sufficient, that some intruder, with the worst intentions, has crept into this honorable company. The ladies present will therefore have the goodness to retire apart to the lower end of the saloon, whilst the noble cavaliers will present themselves in succession to six officers of his Highness's household, to whom they will privately communicate their names and quality."

This arrangement was complied with, not, however, without the exchange of a few flying jests on the part of the younger cavaliers, and their fair partners, as they separated for the purpose. The cavaliers, who were rather more than five hundred in number, went up as they were summoned by the number marked upon their cards of admission, and privately communicating with some one of the officers appointed, were soon told off, and filed away to the right of the Landgrave, waiting for the signal which should give them permission to rejoin their parties.

All had been now told off, within a score. These were clustered together in a group; and in that group undoubtedly was The Masque. Every eye was converged upon this small knot of cavaliers; each of the spectators, according to his fancy, selected the one who came nearest in dress, or in personal appearance, to his preconceptions of that mysterious agent. Not a word was uttered, not a whisper; hardly a robe was heard to rustle, or a feather to wave.

The twenty were rapidly reduced to twelve, these to six, the six to four — three — two ; the tale of the invited was complete, and one man remained behind. That was, past doubting, The Masque !

CHAPTER XVI.

"There stands he that governs Klosterheim by night!" thought every cavalier, as he endeavored to pierce the gloomy being's concealment, with penetrating eyes, or by scrutiny, ten times repeated, to unmasque the dismal secrets which lurked beneath his disguise. "There stands the gloomy murderer!" thought another. "There stands the poor detected criminal," thought the pitying young ladies, "who in the next moment must lay bare his breast to the Landgrave's musketeers."

The figure meantime stood tranquil and collected, apparently not in the least disturbed by the consciousness of his situation, or the breathless suspense of more than a thousand spectators of rank and eminent station, all bending their looks upon himself. He had been leaning against a marble column, as if wrapped up in reverie, and careless of everything about him. But when the dead silence announced that the ceremony was closed, that he only remained to answer for himself, and upon palpable proof — evidence not to be gainsayed — incapable of answering satisfactorily; when in fact it was beyond dispute that here was at length revealed, in bodily presence, before the eyes of those whom he had so long haunted with terrors, The Masque of Klosterheim, — it was naturally expected that now at least he would show alarm and trepidation; that he would prepare for defence, or address himself to instant flight.

Far otherwise! — cooler than any one person beside in the saloon, he stood, like the marble column against which he had been reclining, upright — massy — and imperturbable. He was enveloped in a voluminous mantle, which at this moment, with a leisurely motion, he suffered to fall at his feet, and displayed a figure in which the grace of an Antinous met with the columnar strength of a Grecian Hercules, — presenting, in its *tout ensemble*, the majestic proportions of a Jupiter. He stood — a breathing statue of gladiatorial beauty, towering above all who were near him, and eclipsing the noblest specimens of the human form which the martial assembly presented. A buzz of admiration arose, which in the following moment was suspended by the dubious recollections investing his past appearances, and the terror which waited even on his present movements. He was armed to the teeth; and he was obviously preparing to move.

Not a word had yet been spoken; so tumultuous was the succession of surprises, so mixed and conflicting the feelings, so intense the anxiety. The arrangement of the groups was this; — at the lower half of the room, but starting forward in attitudes of admiration or suspense, were the ladies of Klosterheim. At the upper end, in the centre, one hand raised to bespeak attention, was The Masque of Klosterheim. To his left, and a little behind him, with a subtle Venetian countenance, one hand waving back a half file of musketeers, and the other raised as if to arrest the arm of The Masque, was the wily minister Adorni — creeping nearer and nearer with a stealthy stride. To his right was the great body of Klosterheim cavaliers, a score of students and young officers pressing forward to the front; but in advance of the whole, the Landgrave of X——, haughty, lowering, and throwing out looks of defiance. These were the positions and attitudes in which the first discovery of The Masque had surprised them; and these they still retained. Less dignified spectators were looking downwards from the galleries.

"Surrender!" was the first word by which silence was broken; it came from the Landgrave.

"Or die!" exclaimed Adorni.

"He dies in any case," rejoined the Prince.

The Masque still raised his hand with the action of one who bespeaks attention. Adorni he deigned not to notice. Slightly inclining his head to the Landgrave, in a tone to which it might be the head-dress of elaborate steel-work that gave a sepulchral tone, he replied,—

"The Masque, who rules in Klosterheim by night, surrenders not. He can die. But first he will complete the ceremony of the night, he will reveal himself."

"That is superfluous," exclaimed Adorni; "we need no further revelations. Seize him, and lead him out to death!"

"Dog of an Italian!" replied The Masque, drawing a dag * from his belt, "die first yourself!" And so saying, he slowly turned and levelled the barrel at Adorni, who fled with two bounds to the soldiers in the rear. Then, withdrawing the weapon hastily, he added in a tone of cool contempt, "Or bridle that coward's tongue."

But this was not the minister's intention. "Seize him!" he cried again impetuously to the soldiers, laying his hand on the arm of the foremost, and pointing them forward to their prey.

"No!" said the Landgrave, with a commanding voice; "Halt! I bid you." Something there was in the tone, or it might be that there was something in his private recollections, or something in the general mystery, which promised a discovery that he feared to lose by the too precipitate vengeance of the Italian.

* *Dag*, a sort of pistol or carbine.

"What is it, mysterious being, that you would reveal? Or who is it that you now believe interested in your revelations?"

"Yourself. Prince, it would seem that you have me at your mercy: wherefore, then, the coward haste of this Venetian hound? I am one; you are many. Lead me then out; shoot me. But no: freely I entered this hall; freely I will leave it. If I must die, I will die as a soldier. Such I am; and neither runagate from a foreign land; nor" — turning to Adorni — "a base mechanic."

"But a murderer!" shrieked Adorni: "but a murderer; and with hands yet reeking from innocent blood!"

"Blood, Adorni, that I will yet avenge. Prince, you demand the nature of my revelations. I will reveal my name, my quality, and my mission."

"And to whom?"

"To yourself, and none beside. And, as a pledge for the sincerity of my discoveries, I will first of all communicate a dreadful secret, known, as you fondly believe, to none but your Highness. Prince, dare you receive my revelations?"

Speaking thus, The Masque took one step to the rear, turning his back upon the room, and by a gesture, signified his wish that the Landgrave should accompany him. But at this motion, ten or a dozen of the foremost among the young cavaliers started forward in advance of the Landgrave, in part forming a half circle about his person, and in part commanding the open door-way.

"He is armed!" they exclaimed; "and trebly armed: will your Highness approach him too nearly?"

"I fear him not," said the Landgrave, with something of a contemptuous tone.

"Wherefore should you fear me?" retorted The Masque, with a manner so tranquil and serene as involuntary to disarm suspicion: "Were it possible that I should seek the life of any man here in particular, in that case, (pointing to the fire-arms in his belt,) why should I need to come nearer? Were it possible that any should find in my conduct here a motive to a personal vengeance upon myself, which of you is not near enough? Has your Highness the courage to trample on such terrors?"

Thus challenged as it were to a trial of his courage before the assembled rank of Klosterheim, the Landgrave waved off all who would have stepped forward officiously to his support. If he felt any tremors, he was now sensible that pride and princely honor called upon him to dissemble them. And probably, that sort of tremors, which he felt in reality, did no point in a direct ion to which physical support, such as was now tendered, could have been available. He hesitated no longer, but strode forward to meet The Masque. His highness and The Masque met near the archway of the door, in the very centre of the groups.

With a thrilling tone, deep — piercing — full of alarm, The Masque began thus : —

"To win your confidence, forever to establish credit with your Highness, I will first of all reveal the name of that murderer, who this night dared to pollute your palace with an old man's blood. Prince, bend your ear a little this way."

With a shudder, and a visible effort of self-command, the Landgrave inclined his ear to The Masque, who added, —

"Your Highness will be shocked to hear it:" then, in a lower tone, "Who could have believed it? — It was ———." All was pronounced clearly and strongly, except the last word — the name of the murderer: *that* was made audible only to the Landgrave's ear.

Sudden and tremendous was the effect upon the Prince: he reeled a few paces off; put his hand to the hilt of his sword; smote his forehead; threw frenzied looks upon The Masque, — now half imploring, now dark with vindictive wrath. Then succeeded a pause of profoundest silence, during which all the twelve hundred visitors, whom he had himself assembled, as if expressly to make them witnesses of this extraordinary scene, and of the power with which a stranger could shake him to and fro in a tempestuous strife of passions, were looking and hearkening with senses on the stretch to pierce the veil of silence and of distance. At last the Landgrave mastered his emotions sufficiently to say, "Well, sir, what next?"

"Next comes a revelation of another kind; and I warn you, sir, that it will not be less trying to the nerves. For this first I needed your ear; now I shall need your eyes. Think again, Prince, whether you will stand the trial."

"Pshaw! sir, you trifle with me; again I tell you ——" But here the Landgrave spoke with an affectation of composure and with an effort that did not escape notice; — "again I tell you that I fear you not. Go on."

"Then come forward a little, please your Highness, to the light of this lamp." So saying, with a step or two in advance, he drew the Prince under the powerful glare of a lamp suspended near the great archway of entrance from the interior of the palace. Both were now standing with their faces entirely averted from the spectators. Still more effectually, however, to screen himself from any of those groups on the left, whose advanced position gave them somewhat more the advantage of an oblique aspect, The Masque, at this moment, suddenly drew up, with his left hand, a short Spanish mantle which depended from his shoulders, and now gave him the benefit of a lateral screen. Then, so far as the company behind them could guess at his act, unlocking with his right hand and raising the masque which shrouded his mysterious features, he shouted aloud in a voice that rang clear through every corner of the vast saloon, "Landgrave, for crimes yet unrevealed, I summon you, in twenty days, before a tribunal where there is no shield but innocence!" and at that moment turned his countenance full upon the Prince.

With a yell, rather than a human expression of terror, the Landgrave fell, as if shot by a thunderbolt, stretched at his full length upon the ground, lifeless apparently, and bereft of consciousness or sensation. A sympathetic cry of horror arose from the spectators. All rushed towards The Masque. The young cavaliers, who had first stepped forward as volunteers in the Landgrave's defence, were foremost, and interposed between The Masque and the outstretched arms of Adorni, as if eager to seize him first. In an instant a sudden and dense cloud of smoke arose, nobody knew whence. Repeated discharges of fire-arms were heard resounding from the doorway and the passages; these increased the smoke and the confusion. Trumpets sounded through the corridors. The whole archway, under which The Masque and the Landgrave had been standing, became choked up with soldiery, summoned by the furious alarms that echoed through the palace. All was one uproar and chaos of masques, plumes, helmets, halberds, trumpets, gleaming sabres, and the fierce faces of soldiery forcing themselves through the floating drapery of smoke that now filled the whole upper end of the saloon. Adorni was seen in the midst raving fruitlessly. Nobody heard: nobody listened. Universal panic had seized the household, the soldiery, and the company. Nobody understood exactly for what purpose the tumult had commenced — in what direction it tended. Some tragic catastrophe was reported from mouth to mouth: nobody knew what. Some said, the Landgrave had been assassinated; some, The Masque; some asserted that both had perished under reciprocal assaults. More believed that The Masque had proved to be of that supernatural order of beings, with which the prevailing opinions of Klosterheim had long classed him; and that, upon raising his disguise, he had revealed to the Landgrave, the fleshless skull of some forgotten tenant of the grave. This indeed seemed to many the only solution that, whilst it fell in with the prejudices and superstitions of the age, was of a nature to account for that tremendous effect which the discovery had produced upon the Landgrave. But it was one that naturally could be little calculated to calm the agitations of the public prevailing at this moment. This spread contagiously. The succession of alarming events, — the murder, the appearance of The Masque, his subsequent extraordinary behavior, the overwhelming impression upon the Landgrave, which had formed the catastrophe of this scenical exhibition, — the consternation of the great Swedish officers, who were spending the night in Klosterheim, and reasonably suspected that the tumult might be owing to the sudden detection of their own *incognito*, and that, in consequence, the populace of this Imperial city were suddenly rising to arms; the endless distraction and counteraction of so many thousand persons — visitors, servants, soldiery, household — all hurrying to the same point, and bringing assistance to a danger of which nobody knew the origin, nobody the nature, nobody the issue; multitudes commanding where all obedience was forgotten, all subordination had gone to wreck; — these circumstances of distraction united to sustain a scene of absolute frenzy in the castle, which, for more than half an hour, the dense columns of smoke aggravated alarmingly by raising, in many quarters, additional terrors of fire. And when at last, after infinite exertions, the soldiery had deployed into the ball-room and the adjacent apartments of state, and had succeeded, at the point of the pike, in establishing a safe egress for the twelve hundred visitors, it was then first ascertained that all traces of The Masque had been lost in the smoke and subsequent confusion; and that, with his usual good fortune, he had succeeded in baffling his pursuers.

CHAPTER XVII.

Meantime the Lady Paulina had spent her time in secret grief, inconsolable for the supposed tragical fate of Maximilian. It was believed that he had perished. This opinion had prevailed equally amongst his friends, and the few enemies whom circumstances had made him. Supposing even that he had escaped with life from the action, it seemed inevitable that he should have fallen into the hands of the bloody Holkerstein; and under circumstances which would point him out to the vengeance of that cruel ruffian, as having been the leader in the powerful resistance which had robbed him of his prey.

Stung with the sense of her irreparable loss, and the premature grief which had blighted her early hopes, Paulina sought her refuge in solitude, and her consolations in religion. In the convent, where she had found a home, the ceremonies of the Roman Catholic service were maintained with the strictness and the pomp suitable to its ample endowments. The Emperor had himself, as well as several of his progenitors, been a liberal benefactor to this establishment. And a lady of his house, therefore, recommended by a special introduction from the Emperor to the attentions of the Lady Abbess, was sure of meeting kindness and courtesy in every possible shape which could avail to mitigate her sorrow. The Abbess, though a bigot, was a human being, with strong human sensibilities; and in both characters she was greatly pleased with the Lady Paulina. On the one hand, her pride, as the head of a religious establishment, was flattered by the extreme regularity of the Lady Paulina in conforming to the ritual of her house; this example of spiritual obedience and duty seemed peculiarly edifying in a person of such distinguished rank. On the other hand, her womanly sensibilities were touched by the spectacle of early and unmerited sorrow in one so eminent for her personal merits — for her extreme beauty, and the winning sweetness of her manners. Hence she readily offered to the young Countess all the attentions and marks of sympathy which her retiring habits permitted, and every species of indulgence compatible with the spirit of the institution.

The whole convent, nuns as well as strangers, taking their tone from the Abbess, vied with each other in attentions to Paulina. But, whilst acknowledging their kindness, she continued to shrink from all general intercourse with the society about her. Her attendance was constant at the matins and at vespers ; not unfrequently even at the midnight service ; but dejection was too rooted in her heart, to allow her any disposition to enter into the amusements or mixed society which the convent at that time offered.

Many noble strangers had been allowed to take up their quarters in the convent. With some of these the Abbess was connected by blood, with others, by ties of ancient friendship. Most of this party composed a little society apart from the rest, and continued to pursue those amusements or occupations which properly belonged to their stations and quality, but by their too worldly nature, were calculated to exclude the religious members of the institution from partaking in them. To this society, Paulina received frequent invitations, which, however, she declined so uniformly, that at length all efforts ceased to draw her from the retirement which she so manifestly adhered to from choice. The motives of her dejection became known throughout the convent, and were respected ; and it was now reported amongst them, from her aversion to society as well as her increasing devotion, that the Lady Paulina would soon take the veil.

Amongst the strangers was one, a lady of mature age, with beauty still powerful enough to fascinate all beholders, who seemed to survey Paulina with an interest far beyond that of curiosity or simple admiration. Sorrow might be supposed the common bond which connected them ; for there were rumors amongst the sisterhood of St. Agnes that this lady had suffered afflictions heavier than fell to an ordinary lot in the course of the war which now desolated Germany. Her husband, (it was said,) of whom no more was known than that he was some officer of high rank, had perished by the hand of violence ; a young daughter, the only child of two or three who remained to her, had been carried off in infancy ; and no traces remained of her subsequent fate. To these misfortunes was added the loss of her estates and rank, which, in some mysterious way, were supposed to be withheld from her by one of those great oppressors whom war and the policy of great allies had aggrandized. It was supposed even that for the means of subsistence to herself, and a few faithful attendants, she was indebted to the kindness of the Lady Abbess, with whom she was closely connected by ancient friendship.

In this tale there were many inaccuracies mixed up with the truth. It was true that, in some one of the many dire convulsions which had passed from land to land since the first outbreak of the Bohemian troubles, in 1618, and which had covered with a veil of political pretexts so many local acts of private family feud and murderous treason, this lady had been deprived of her husband by a violent death under circumstances which still seemed mysterious. But the fate of her children, if any had survived the calamity which took off her husband, was unknown to everybody except her confidential protectress the Lady Abbess. By permission of this powerful friend, who had known her from infancy and through the whole course of her misfortunes, she was permitted to take up her abode in the convent, under special privileges, and was there known by the name of Sister Madeline.

The intercourse of the Sister Madeline with the Lady Abbess was free and unreserved. At all hours they entered each other's rooms with the familiarity of sisters; and it might have been thought that in every respect they stood upon the equal footing of near relatives, except that occasionally in the manners of the Abbess was traced or imagined a secret air of deference towards the desolate Sister Madeline, which, as it was not countenanced at all by their present relations to each other, left people at liberty to build upon it a large superstructure of romantic conjectures.

Sister Madeline was as regular in her attendance upon prayers as Paulina. There, if nowhere else, they were sure of meeting; and in no long time it became evident that the younger lady was an object of particular interest to the elder. When the sublime fugues of the old composers for the organ swelled upon the air, and filled the vast aisles of the chapel with their floating labyrinths of sound, attention to the offices of the church service being suspended for the time, the Sister Madeline spent the interval in watching the countenance of Paulina. Invariably at this period her eyes settled upon the young Countess, and appeared to court some return of attention, by the tender sympathy which her own features expressed with the grief too legibly inscribed upon Paulina's. For some time Paulina, absorbed by her own thoughts, failed to notice this very particular expression of attention and interest. Accustomed to the gaze of crowds, as well on account of her beauty as her connection with the Imperial house, she found nothing new or distressing in this attention to herself. After some time, however, observing herself still haunted by the sister's furtive glances, she found her own curiosity somewhat awakened in return. The manners of Sister Madeline were too dignified, and her face expressed too much of profound feeling, and traces too inextinguishable of the trials through which she had passed, to allow room for any belief that she was under the influence of an ordinary curiosity. Paulina was struck with a confused feeling, that she looked upon features which had already been familiar to her heart, though disguised in Sister Madeline by age, by sex, and by the ravages of grief; she had the appearance of having passed her fiftieth year; but it was probable that, spite of a brilliant complexion, secret sorrow had worked a natural effect in giving to her the appearance of age more advanced by seven or eight years than she had really attained. Time at all events, if it had carried off forever her youthful graces, neither had nor seemed likely to destroy the impression of majestic beauty under eclipse and wane. No one could fail to read the signs by which the finger of nature announces a great destiny, and a mind born to command.

Insensibly the two ladies had established a sort of intercourse by looks ; and at length, upon finding that the Sister Madeline mixed no more than herself in the general society of Klosterheim, Paulina had resolved to seek the acquaintance of a lady whose deportment announced that she would prove an interesting acquaintance, whilst her melancholy story and the expression of her looks were a sort of pledges that she would be found a sympathizing friend.

She had already taken some steps towards the attainment of her wishes, when unexpectedly, on coming out from the vesper service, the Sister Madeline placed herself by the side of Paulina, and they walked down one of the long side aisles together. The saintly memorials about them, the records of everlasting peace which lay sculptured at their feet, and the strains which still ascended to heaven from the organ and the white-robed choir, — all speaking of a rest from trouble so little to be found on earth, and so powerfully contrasting with the desolations of poor harassed Germany, — affected them deeply, and both burst into tears. At length the elderly lady spoke.

"Daughter, you keep your faith piously with him whom you suppose dead."

Paulina started. The other continued —

"Honor to young hearts that are knit together by ties so firm that even death has no power to dissolve them! Honor to the love which can breed so deep a sorrow! Yet, even in this world, the good are not *always* the unhappy. I doubt not that, even now at vespers, you forgot not to pray for him that would willingly have died for you."

"Oh, gracious lady! when — when have I forgot that? What other prayer — what other image — is ever at my heart?"

"Daughter, I could not doubt it; and Heaven sometimes sends answers to prayers when they are least expected; and to yours it sends this through me."

With these words she stretched out a letter to Paulina, who fainted with sudden surprise and delight on recognizing the hand of Maximilian.

CHAPTER XVIII.

It was indeed the handwriting of her lover; and the first words of the letter, which bore a recent date, announced his safety and his recovered health. A rapid sketch of all which had befallen him since they had last parted, informed her that he had been severely wounded in the action with Holkerstein's people, and probably to that misfortune had been indebted for his life, since the difficulty of transporting him on horseback, when unable to sit upright, had compelled the party charged with his care to leave him for the night at Waldenhausen. From that place he had been carried off in the night-time to a small Imperial garrison in the neighborhood by the care of two faithful servants, who had found little difficulty in first intoxicating, and then overpowering, the small guard judged sufficient for a prisoner so completely disabled by his wounds. In this garrison he had recovered; had corresponded with Vienna; had concerted measures with the Emperor; and was now on the point of giving full effect to their plans, at the moment when certain circumstances should arise to favor the scheme. What these were, he forbore designedly to say in a letter which ran some risk of falling into the enemy's hands; but he bade Paulina speedily to expect a great change for the better, which would put it in their power to meet without restraint or fear, — and concluded by giving utterance in the fondest terms to a lover's hopes and tenderest anxieties.

Paulina had scarcely recovered from the tumultuous sensations of pleasure, and sudden restoration to hope, when she received a shock in the opposite direction, from a summons to attend the Landgrave. The language of the message was imperative, and more peremptory than had ever before been addressed to herself, a lady of the Imperial family. She knew the Landgrave's character and his present position: both these alarmed her, when connected with the style and language of his summons. For *that* announced distinctly enough that his resolution had been now taken to commit himself to a bold course, no longer to hang doubtfully between two policies, but openly to throw himself into the arms of the Emperor's enemies. In one view, Paulina found a benefit to her spirits from this haughtiness of the Landgrave's message. She was neither proud, nor apt to take offence. On the contrary, she was gentle and meek; for the impulses of youth and elevated birth had in her been chastened by her early acquaintance with great national calamities, and the enlarged sympathy which that had bred with her fellow-creatures of every rank. But she felt that, in this superfluous expression of authority, the Landgrave was at the same time infringing the rights of hospitality, and her own privileges of sex. Indignation at his unmanly conduct gave her spirits to face him, though she apprehended a scene of violence, and had the more reason to feel the trepidations of uncertainty, because she very imperfectly comprehended his purposes as respected herself.

These were not easily explained. She found the Landgrave pacing the room with violence. His back was turned towards her as she entered; but as the usher announced loudly on her entrance, "The Countess Paulina of Hohenhelder," he turned impetuously, and advanced to meet her. With the Landgrave, however irritated, the first impulse was to comply with the ceremonious observances that belonged to his rank. He made a cold obeisance, whilst an attendant placed a seat; and then motioning to all present to withdraw, began to unfold the causes which had called for Lady Paulina's presence.

So much art was mingled with so much violence, that for some time Paulina gathered nothing of his real purposes. Resolved, however, to do justice to her own insulted dignity, she took the first opening which offered, to remonstrate with the Landgrave on the needless violence of his summons. His Serene

Highness wielded the sword in Klosterheim, and could have no reason for anticipating resistance to his commands.

"The Lady Paulina then distinguishes between the power and the right? I expected as much."

"By no means; she knew nothing of the claimants to either. She was a stranger, seeking only hospitality in Klosterheim, which apparently was violated by unprovoked exertions of authority."

"But the laws of hospitality," replied the Landgrave, "press equally on the guest and the host. Each has his separate duties. And the Lady Paulina, in the character of guest, violated her's from the moment when she formed cabals in Klosterheim, and ministered to the fury of conspirators."

"Your ear, sir, is abused; I have not so much as stepped beyond the precincts of the convent in which I reside, until this day in paying obedience to your Highness's mandate."

"That may be; and that may argue only the more caution and subtlety. The personal presence of a lady, so distinguished in her appearance as the Lady Paulina, at any resort of conspirators or intriguers, would have published too much the suspicions to which such a countenance would be liable. But in writing, have you dispersed nothing calculated to alienate the attachment of my subjects?"

The Lady Paulina shook her head; she knew not

even in what direction the Landgrave's suspicions pointed.

"As, for example, this — does the Lady Paulina recognize this particular paper?"

Saying this, he drew forth from a portfolio a letter or paper of instructions, consisting of several sheets, to which a large official seal was attached. The Countess glanced her eye over it attentively; in one or two places the words *Maximilian* and *Klosterheim* attracted her attention; but she felt satisfied at once that she now saw it for the first time.

"Of this paper," she said at length, in a determined tone, "I know nothing. The handwriting I believe I may have seen before. It resembles that of one of the Emperor's secretaries. Beyond that, I have no means of even conjecturing its origin."

"Beware, madam, beware how far you commit yourself. Suppose, now, this paper were actually brought in one of your ladyship's mails, amongst your own private property."

"That may very well be," said Lady Paulina, "and yet imply no falsehood on my part. Falsehood! I disdain such an insinuation; your Highness has been the first person who ever dared to make it." At that moment she called to mind the robbery of her carriage at Waldenhausen. Coloring deeply with indignation, she added, "Even in the case, sir, which you have supposed, as unconscious bearer of this or any other paper, I am still innocent of the intentions which such an act might argue in some people. I am as incapable of offending in that way, as I shall always be of disavowing any of my own acts, according to your ungenerous insinuation. But now, sir, tell me how far those may be innocent who have possessed themselves of a paper carried, as your Highness alleges, among my private baggage? Was it for a Prince to countenance a robbery of that nature, or to appropriate its spoils?"

The blood rushed to the Landgrave's temples. "In these times, young lady, petty rights of individuals give way to state necessities. Neither are there any such rights of individuals in bar of such an inquisition. They are forfeited, as I told you before, when the guest forgets his duties. "But," (and here he frowned) "it seems to me, Countess, that you are now forgetting your situation; not I, remember, but yourself, are now placed on trial."

"Indeed!" said the Countess, "of that I was certainly not aware. Who, then, is my accuser, who my judge? Or is it in your Serene Highness that I see both?"

"Your accuser, Lady Paulina, is the paper I have shown you, a treasonable paper. Perhaps I have others to bring forward of the same bearing. Perhaps this is sufficient."

The Lady Paulina grew suddenly sad and thoughtful.

Here was a tyrant, with matter against her, which, even to an unprejudiced judge, might really wear some face of plausibility. The paper had, perhaps, really been one of those plundered from her carriage. It might really contain matter fitted to excite disaffection against the Landgrave's government. Her own innocence of all participation in the designs which it purported to abet might find no credit, or might avail her not at all in a situation so far removed from the Imperial protection. She had in fact unadvisedly entered a city which, at the time of her entrance, might be looked upon as neutral, but since then she had been forced into the ranks of the Emperor's enemies too abruptly to allow of warning or retreat. This was her exact situation. She saw her danger, and again apprehended that, at the very moment of recovering her lover from the perils besetting *his* situation, she might lose him by the perils of her own.

The Landgrave watched the changes of her countenance, and read her thoughts.

"Yes," he said at length, "your situation is one of peril. But take courage. Confess freely, and you have everything to hope for from my clemency."

"Such clemency," said a deep voice, from some remote quarter of the room, "as the wolf shows to the lamb."

Paulina started, and the Landgrave looked angry and perplexed. "Within there!" he cried loudly to his attendants in the next room. "I will no more endure these insults," he exclaimed. "Go instantly, take a file of soldiers; place them at all the outlets, and search the rooms adjoining — above and below. Such mummery is insufferable."

The voice replied again, "Landgrave, you search in vain. Look to yourself! young Max is upon you!"

"This babbler," said the Landgrave, making an effort to recover his coolness, "reminds me well; that adventurer, young Maximilian — who is he, whence comes he? by whom authorized?"

Paulina blushed; but, roused by the Landgrave's contumelious expressions applied to her lover, she replied — "He is no adventurer; nor was ever in that class; the Emperor's favor is not bestowed upon such."

"Then, what brings him to Klosterheim? For what is it that he would trouble the repose of this city?"

Before Paulina could speak in rejoinder, the voice, from a little further distance, replied audibly — "For his rights! See that you, Landgrave, make no resistance."

The Prince arose in fury; his eyes flashed fire; he clenched his hands in impotent determination. The same voice had annoyed him on former occasions, but never under circumstances which mortified him so deeply. Ashamed that the youthful Countess should be a witness of the insults put upon him, and seeing that it was in vain to pursue his conversation with her further in a situation which exposed him to the sarcasms of a third person, under no restraint of fear or partiality, he adjourned the further prosecution of his inquiry to another opportunity, and for the present gave her leave to depart; a license which she gladly availed herself of, and retired in fear and perplexity.

CHAPTER XIX.

It was dark as Paulina returned to her convent. Two servants of the Landgrave's preceded her with torches to the great gates of St. Agnes, which was at a very short distance. At that point she entered within the shelter of the convent gates, and the Prince's servants left her at her own request. No person was now within call but a little page of her own, and perhaps the porter at the convent. But after the first turn in the garden of St. Agnes, she might almost consider herself as left to her own guardianship; for the little boy who followed her was too young to afford her any effectual help. She felt sorry, as she surveyed the long avenue of ancient trees, which was yet to be traversed before she entered upon the cloisters, that she should have dismissed the servants of the Landgrave. These gardens were easily scaled from the outside, and a ready communication existed between the remotest parts of this very avenue, and some of the least reputable parts of Klosterheim. The city now overflowed with people of every rank; and amongst them were continually recognized, and occasionally challenged, some of the vilest deserters from the Imperial camps. Wallenstein himself, and other Imperial commanders, but, above all, Holk, had attracted to their standards the very refuse of the German jails; and allowing an unlimited license of plunder during some periods of their career, had themselves evoked a fiendish spirit of lawless aggression and spoliation, which afterwards they had found it impossible to exorcise within its former limits. People were everywhere obliged to be on their guard, not alone (as heretofore) against the military tyrant or freebooter, but also against the private servants whom they hired into their service. For some time back, suspicious persons had been seen strolling at dusk in the gardens of St. Agnes, or even intruding into the cloisters. Then the recollection of The Masque, now in the very height of his mysterious career, flashed upon Paulina's thoughts. Who knew his motives, or the principles of his mysterious warfare — which at any rate, in its mode, had latterly been marked by bloodshed? As these things came rapidly into her mind, she trembled more from fear than from the wintry wind, which now blew keenly and gustily through the avenue.

The gardens of St. Agnes were extensive, and Paulina yet wanted two hundred yards of reaching the cloisters, when she observed a dusky object stealing along the margin of a little pool, which in parts lay open to the walk, whilst in others, where the walk receded from the water, the banks were studded with thickets of tall shrubs. Paulina stopped and observed the figure, which she was soon satisfied must be that of a man. At times he rose to his full height; at times he cowered downwards amongst the bushes. That he was not merely seeking a retreat, became evident from this, that the best road for such a purpose lay open to him in the opposite direction; — that he was watching herself, also, became probable from the way in which he seemed to regulate his own motions by her's. At length, whilst Paulina hesitated in some perplexity whether to go forward or to retreat towards the porter's lodge, he suddenly plunged into the thickest belt of shrubs, and left the road clear. Paulina seized the moment, and with a palpitating heart quickened her steps towards the cloister.

She had cleared about one-half of the way without obstruction, when suddenly a powerful grasp seized her by the shoulder.

"Stop, lady!" said a deep, coarse voice, "stop! I mean no harm. Perhaps I bring your ladyship what will be welcome news."

"But why here?" exclaimed Paulina; "wherefore do you alarm me thus? Oh! heavens! your eyes are wild and fierce; say, is it money that you want?"

"Perhaps I do. To the like of me, lady, you may be sure that money never comes amiss; — but that is not my errand. Here is what will make all clear;" and, as he spoke, he thrust his hand into the huge pocket within the horseman's cloak which enveloped him. Instead of the pistol or dag, which Paulina anticipated, he drew forth a large packet, carefully sealed. Paulina felt so much relieved at beholding this pledge of the man's pacific intentions, that she eagerly pressed her purse into his hand, and was hastening to leave him, when the man stopped her to deliver a verbal message from his master, requesting earnestly that, if she concluded to keep the appointment arranged in the letter, she would not be a minute later than the time fixed.

"And who," said Paulina, "is your master?"

"Surely the General, madam — the young General Maximilian. Many a time and oft have I waited on him when visiting your ladyship at the Wartebrunn. But here I dare not show my face. Der Henker! if the Landgrave knew that Michael Klotz was in Klosterheim, I reckon that all the ladies in St. Agnes could not beg him a reprieve till to-morrow morning."

"Then, villain!" said the foremost of two men who rushed hastily from the adjoining shrubs, "be assured that the Landgrave does know it. Let this be your warrant!" With these words he fired, and, immediately after, his comrade. Whether the fugitive were wounded could not be known; for he instantly plunged into the water, and, after two or three moments, was heard upon the opposite margin. His pursuers seemed to shrink from this attempt, for they divided and took the opposite extremities of the pool, from the other bank of which they were soon heard animating and directing each other through the darkness.

Paulina, confused and agitated, and anxious above all to examine her letters, took the opportunity of a clear road, and fled in trepidation to the convent.

CHAPTER XX.

The Countess had brought home with her a double subject of anxiety. She knew not to what result the Landgrave's purposes were tending; she feared, also, from this sudden and new method of communication opened with herself so soon after his previous letter, that some unexpected bad fortune might now be threatening her lover. Hastily she tore open the packet, which manifestly contained something larger than letters. The first article which presented itself was a nun's veil, exactly on the pattern of those worn by the nuns of St. Agnes. The accompanying letter sufficiently explained its purpose.

It was in the handwriting, and bore the signature, of Maximilian. In a few words he told her that a sudden communication, but from a quarter entirely to be depended on, had reached him of a great danger impending over her from the Landgrave; that in the present submission of Klosterheim to that Prince's will, instant flight presented the sole means of delivering her; for which purpose he would himself meet her in disguise on the following morning, as early as four o'clock; or, if that should prove impossible under the circumstances of the case, would send a faithful servant: — that one or other of them would attend at a particular station, easily recognized by the description added, in a ruinous part of the boundary wall, in the rear of the convent garden. A large travelling cloak would be brought to draw over the rest of her dress; but meanwhile, as a means of passing unobserved through the convent grounds, where the Landgrave's agents were continually watching her motions, the nun's veil was almost indispensable. The other circumstances of the journey would be communicated to her upon meeting. In conclusion, the writer implored Paulina to suffer no scruples of false delicacy to withhold her from a step which had so suddenly become necessary to her preservation; and cautioned her particularly against communicating her intentions to the Lady Abbess, whose sense of decorum might lead her to urge advice at this moment inconsistent with her safety.

Again and again did Paulina read this agitating letter; again and again did she scrutinize the handwriting, apprehensive that she might be making herself a dupe to some hidden enemy. The handwriting, undoubtedly, had not all the natural freedom which characterized that of Maximilian — it was somewhat stiff in its movement, but not more so than that of his previous letter, in which he had accounted for the slight change from a wound not perfectly healed in his right hand. In other respects, the letter seemed liable to no just suspicion. The danger apprehended from the Landgrave tallied with her own knowledge. The convent grounds were certainly haunted, as the letter alleged, by the Landgrave's people, — of that she had just received a convincing proof; for, though the two strangers had turned off in pursuit of the messenger who bore Maximilian's letter, yet doubtless their original object of attention had been herself; they were then posted to watch her motions, and they had avowed themselves in effect the Landgrave's people. That part of the advice, again, which respected the Lady Abbess, seemed judicious, on considering the character of that lady, however much at first sight it might warrant some jealousy of the writer's purposes, to find him warning her against her best friends. After all, what most disturbed the confidence of Paulina was the countenance of the man who presented the letter; if this man were to be the representative of Maximilian on the following morning, she felt, and was persuaded that she would continue to feel, an invincible repugnance to commit her safety to any such keeping. Upon the whole, she resolved to keep the appointment, but to be guided in her further conduct by circumstances as they should arise at the moment.

That night Paulina's favorite female attendant employed herself in putting into as small a compass as possible the slender wardrobe which they would be able to carry with them. The young Countess herself spent the hours in writing to the Lady Abbess and Sister Madeline, acquainting them with all the circumstances of her interview with the Landgrave, — the certain grounds she had for apprehending some great danger in that quarter, — and the proposals so unexpectedly made to her on the part of Maximilian for evading it. To ask that they should feel no anxiety on her account, in times which made even a successful escape from danger so very hazardous, she acknowledged would be in vain; but, in judging of the degree of prudence which she had exhibited on this occasion, she begged them to reflect on the certain dangers which awaited her from the Landgrave; and finally, in excuse for not having sought the advice of so dear a friend as the Lady Abbess, she enclosed the letter upon which she had acted.

These preparations were completed by midnight, after which Paulina sought an hour or two of repose. At three o'clock were celebrated the early matins, attended by the devouter part of the sisterhood, in the chapel. Paulina and her maid took this opportunity for leaving their chamber, and slipping unobserved amongst the crowd who were hurrying on that summons into the cloisters. The organ was pealing solemnly through the labyrinth of passages which led from the interior of the convent; and Paulina's eyes were suffused with tears, as the gentler recollections of her earlier days, and the peace which belongs to those who have abjured this world and its treacherous promises, arose to her mind, under the influence of the sublime music, in powerful contrast with the tempestuous troubles of Germany — now become so comprehensive in their desolating sweep, as to involve even herself, and others of station as elevated.

CHAPTER XXI.

The convent clock, chiming the quarters, at length announced that they had reached the appointed hour. Trembling with fear and cold, though muffled up in furs, Paulina and her attendant, with their nuns' veils drawn over their head-dress, sallied forth into the garden. All was profoundly dark, and overspread with the stillness of the grave. The lights within the chapel threw a rich glow through the painted window; and here and there, from a few scattered casements in the vast pile of St. Agnes, streamed a few weak rays from a taper or a lamp, indicating the trouble of a sick-bed, or the peace of prayer. But these rare lights did but deepen the massy darkness of all beside; and Paulina, with her attendant, had much difficulty in making her way to the appointed station. Having reached the wall, however, they pursued its windings, certain of meeting no important obstacles, until they attained a part where their progress was impeded by frequent dilapidations. Here they halted, and in low tones communicated their doubts about the precise locality of the station indicated in the letter, when suddenly a man started up from the ground, and greeted them with the words, "St. Agnes! all is right," which had been preconcerted as the signal in the letter. This man was courteous and respectful in his manner of speaking, and had nothing of the ruffian voice which belonged to the bearer of the letter. In rapid terms he assured Paulina, that "the Young General" had not found circumstances favorable for venturing within the walls, but that he would meet her a few miles beyond the city gates; and that at present they had no time to lose. Saying this, he unshaded a dark lantern, which showed them a ladder of ropes, attached to the summit of a wall, which at this point was too low to occasion them much uneasiness or difficulty in ascending. But Paulina insisted previously on hearing something more circumstantial of the manner and style of their escape from the city walls, and in what company their journey would be performed. The man had already done something to conciliate Paulina's confidence by the propriety of his address, which indicated a superior education, and habits of intercourse with people of rank. He explained as much of the plan as seemed necessary for the immediate occasion. A convoy of arms and military stores was leaving the city for the post at Falkenstein. Several carriages, containing privileged persons, to whom the Landgrave or his minister had granted a license, were taking the benefit of an escort over the forest; and a bribe in the proper quarter had easily obtained permission, from the officer on duty at the gates, to suffer an additional carriage to pass as one in a great lady's suite, on the simple condition that it should contain none but females; as persons of that sex were liable to no suspicion of being fugitives from the wrath which was now supposed ready to descend upon the conspirators against the Landgrave.

This explanation reconciled Paulina to the scheme. She felt cheered by the prospect of having other ladies to countenance the mode of her nocturnal journey; and at the worst, hearing this renewed mention of conspirators and punishment, which easily connected itself with all that had passed in her interview with the Landgrave, she felt assured, at any rate, that the dangers she fled from, transcended any which she was likely to incur upon her route. Her determination was immediately taken. She passed over the wall with her attendant; and they found themselves in a narrow lane, close to the city walls, with none but a few ruinous outhouses on either side. A low whistle from the man was soon answered by the rumbling of wheels; and from some distance, as it seemed, a sort of caleche advanced, drawn by a pair of horses. Paulina and her attendant stepped hastily in, for at the very moment when the carriage drew up, a signal gun was heard; which, as their guide assured them, proclaimed that the escort and the whole train of carriages were at that moment defiling from the city gate. The driver, obeying the directions of the other man, drove off as rapidly as the narrow road and the darkness would allow. A few turns brought them into the great square in front of the *schloss;* from which, a few more open streets, traversed at full gallop, soon brought them into the rear of the convoy, which had been unexpectedly embarrassed in its progress to the gate. From the rear, by dexterous management, they gradually insinuated themselves into the centre; and, contrary to their expectations, amongst the press of baggage-wagons, artillery, and travelling equipages, all tumultuously clamoring to push on, as the best chance of evading Holkerstein in the forest, their own unpretending vehicle passed without other notice than a curse from the officer on duty; which, however, they could not presume to appropriate, as it might be supposed equitably distributed amongst all who stopped the road at the moment.

Paulina shuddered as she looked out upon the line of fierce faces, illuminated by the glare of torches, and mingling with horses' heads, and the gleam of sabres; all around her, the roar of artillery wheels; above her head, the vast arch of the gates, its broad massy shadows resting below; and in the vista beyond, which the archway defined, a mass of blackness in which she rather imagined than saw the interminable solitudes of the forest. Soon the gate was closed; their own carriage passed the tardier parts of the convoy; and, with a dozen or two of others, surrounded by a squadron of dragoons, headed the train. Happy beyond measure at the certainty that she had now cleared the gates of Klosterheim, that she was in the wide open forest — free from a detested tyrant, and on the same side of the gates as her lover, who was doubtless advancing to meet her — she threw herself back in the carriage, and resigned herself to a slumber, which the anxieties and watchings of the night had made more than usually welcome.

The city clocks were now heard in the forest, solemnly knelling out the hour of four. Hardly, however, had Paulina slept an hour, when she was gently awakened by her attendant — who had felt it to be her duty to apprise her lady of the change which had occurred in their situation. They had stopped, it seemed, to attach a pair of leaders to their wheel horses; and were now advancing at a thundering pace, separated from the rest of the convoy, and surrounded by a small escort of cavalry. The darkness was still intense; and the lights of Klosterheim, which the frequent windings of the road brought often into view, were at this moment conspicuously seen. The castle, from its commanding position, and the convent of St. Agnes, were both easily traced out by means of the lights gleaming from their long ranges of upper windows. A particular turret, which sprang to an almost aerial altitude above the rest of the building, in which it was generally reported that the Landgrave slept, was more distinguishable than any other part of Klosterheim, from one brilliant lustre which shot its rays through a large oriel window. There at this moment was sleeping that unhappy prince, tyrannical and self-tormenting, whose unmanly fears had menaced her own innocence with so much indefinite danger; whom, in escaping, she knew not if she *had* escaped; and whose snares, as a rueful misgiving began to suggest, were perhaps gathering faster about her, with every echo which the startled forest returned to the resounding tread of their flying cavalcade. She leaned back again in the carriage; again she fell asleep; again she dreamed. But her sleep was unrefreshing; her dreams were agitated, confused, and haunted by terrific images. And she awoke repeatedly with her cheerful anticipation, continually decaying, of speedily (perhaps ever again) rejoining her gallant Maximilian. There was indeed yet a possibility that she might be under the superintending care of her lover. But she secretly felt that she was betrayed. And she wept when she reflected that her own precipitance had facilitated the accomplishment of the plot which had perhaps forever ruined her happiness.

CHAPTER XXI.

MEANTIME, Paulina awoke from the troubled slumbers into which her fatigues had thrown her, to find herself still flying along as rapidly as four powerful horses could draw their light burden, and still escorted by a considerable body of the Landgrave's dragoons. She was undoubtedly separated from all the rest of the convoy, with whom she had left Klosterheim. It was now apparent, even to her humble attendant, that they were betrayed; and Paulina reproached herself with having voluntarily co-operated with her enemy's stratagems. Certainly the dangers from which she fled were great and imminent; yet still, in Klosterheim, she derived some protection from the favor of the Lady Abbess. That lady had great powers of a legal nature throughout the city, and still greater influence with a Roman Catholic populace at this particular period, when their Prince had laid himself open to suspicions of favoring Protestant allies; and Paulina bitterly bewailed the imprudence, which, in removing her from the convent of St. Agnes, had removed her from her only friends.

It was about noon, when the party halted at a solitary house for rest and refreshments. Paulina had heard nothing of the route which they had hitherto taken, nor did she find it easy to collect, from the short and churlish responses of her escort to the few questions she had yet ventured to propose, in what direction their future advance would proceed. A hasty summons bade her alight; and a few steps, under the guidance of a trooper, brought her into a little gloomy wainscoted room, where some refreshments had been already spread upon a table. Adjoining was a small bed-room. And she was desired, with something more of civility than she had yet experienced, to consider both as allotted for the use of herself and servant during the time of their stay, which was expected, however, not to exceed the two or three hours requisite for resting the horses.

But that was an arrangement which depended as much upon others as themselves. And in fact a small party, whom the main body of the escort had sent on to patrol the roads in advance, soon returned with the unwelcome news that a formidable corps of Imperialists were out reconnoitring in a direction which might probably lead them across their own line of march, in the event of their proceeding instantly. The orders already issued for advance were therefore countermanded; and a resolution was at length adopted by the leader of the party for taking up their abode during the night in their present very tolerable quarters.

Paulina, wearied and dejected, and recoiling naturally from the indefinite prospects of danger before her, was not the least rejoiced at this change in the original plan, by which she benefited at any rate to the extent of a quiet shelter for one night more, a blessing which the next day's adventures might deny her, and still more by that postponement of impending evil which is so often welcome to the very firmest minds, when exhausted by toil and affliction. Having this certainty, however, of one night's continuance in her present abode, she requested to have the room made a little more comfortable by the exhilarating blaze of a fire. For this indulgence there were the principal requisites in a hearth and spacious chimney. And an aged crone, probably the sole female servant upon the premises, speedily presented herself with a plentiful supply of wood, and the two supporters, or *andirons* (as they were formerly called), for raising the billets so as to allow the air to circulate from below. There was some difficulty at first in kindling the wood; and the old servant resorted once or twice, after some little apologetic muttering of doubts with herself, to a closet, containing, as Paulina could observe, a considerable body of papers.

The fragments which she left remained strewed upon the ground: and Paulina, taking them up with a careless air, was suddenly transfixed with astonishment on observing that they were undoubtedly in a handwriting familiar to her eye — the handwriting of the most confidential amongst the Imperial secretaries. Other recollections now rapidly associated themselves together, which led her hastily to open the closet door; and there, as she had already half expected, she saw the travelling mail stolen from her own carriage, its lock forced, and the remaining contents (for everything bearing a money value had probably vanished on its first disappearance) lying in confusion. Having made this discovery, she hastily closed the door of the closet, resolved to prosecute her investigations in the night-time; but at present, when she was liable to continual intrusions, to give no occasion for those suspicions, which, once aroused, might end in baffling her design.

Meantime she occupied herself in conjectures upon the particular course of accident which could have brought the trunk and papers into the situation where she had been fortunate enough to find them. And with the clue already in her possession, she was not long in making another discovery; she had previously felt some dim sense of recognition, as her eyes wandered over the room; but had explained it away into some resemblance into one or other of the many strange scenes which she had passed through since leaving Vienna. But now, on retracing the furniture and aspect of the two rooms, she was struck with her own inattention, in not having sooner arrived at the discovery, that it was their old quarters of Waldenhausen, the very place in which the robbery had been effected, where they had again the prospect of spending the night, and of recovering in part the loss she had sustained.

Midnight came, and the Lady Paulina prepared to avail herself of her opportunities. She drew out the parcel of papers, which was large and miscellaneous in its contents. By far the greater part, as she was happy to observe, were mere copies of originals in the chancery at Vienna; those related to the civic affairs of Klosterheim, and were probably of a nature not to have been acted upon during the predominance of the Swedish interest in the counsels and administration of that city. With the revival of the Imperial cause, no doubt these orders would be repeated, and with the modifications which new circumstances, and the progress of events, would then have rendered expedient. This portion of the papers, therefore, Paulina willingly restored to their situation in the closet. No evil would arise to any party from their present detention in a place where they were little likely to attract notice from any body, but the old lady in her ministries upon the fire. Suspicion would be also turned aside from herself in appropriating the few papers which remained. These contained too frequent mention of a name dear to herself, not to have a considerable value in her eyes; she was resolved, if possible, to carry them off by concealing them within her bosom; but at all events, in preparation for any misfortune that might ultimately compel her to resign them, she determined without loss of time to make herself mistress of their contents.

One, and the most important of these documents, was a long and confidential letter from the Emperor to the Town-Council and the chief heads of conventual houses in Klosterheim. It contained a rapid summary of the principal events in her lover's life, from his infancy, when some dreadful domestic tragedy had thrown him upon the Emperor's protection, to his present period of early manhood, when his own sword and distinguished talents had raised him to a brilliant name and a high military rank in the Imperial service. What were the circumstances of that tragedy, as a case sufficiently well known to those whom he addressed, or to be collected from accompanying papers, the Emperor did not say. But he lavished every variety of praise upon Maximilian, with a liberality that won tears of delight from the solitary young lady, as she now sat at midnight looking over these gracious testimonies to her lover's merit. A theme, so delightful to Paulina, could not be unseasonable at any time; and never did her thoughts revert to him more fondly than at this moment, when she so much needed his protecting arm. Yet, the Emperor, she was aware, must have some more special motive for enlarging upon this topic, than his general favor to Maximilian. What this could be in a case so closely connecting the parties to the correspondence on both sides with Klosterheim, a little interested her curiosity. And, on looking more narrowly at the accompanying documents, in one which had been most pointedly referred to by the Emperor, she found some disclosures on the subject of her lover's early misfortunes, which, whilst they filled her with horror and astonishment, elevated the natural pretensions of Maximilian in point of birth and descent more nearly to a level with the splendor of his self-created distinctions; and thus crowned him, who already lived in her apprehension as the very model of a hero, with the only advantages that he had ever been supposed to want — the interest which attaches to unmerited misfortunes, and the splendor of an illustrious descent.

As she thus sat, absorbed in the story of her lover's early misfortunes, a murmuring sound of talking attracted her ear, apparently issuing from the closet. Hastily throwing open the door, she found that a thin wooden partition, veined with numerous chinks, was the sole separation between the closet and an adjoining bed-room. The words were startling, incoherent, and at times raving. Evidently they proceeded from some patient stretched on a bed of sickness, and dealing with a sort of horrors in his distempered fancy, worse, it was to be hoped, than any which the records of his own remembrance could bring before him. Sometimes he spoke in the character of one who chases a deer in a forest; sometimes he was close upon the haunches of his game; sometimes it seemed on the point of escaping him. Then the nature of the game changed utterly, and became something human; and a companion was suddenly at his side. With him he quarrelled fiercely about their share in the pursuit and capture. "Oh, my lord, you must not deny it. Look, look! your hands are bloodier than mine. Fie! fie! is there no running water in the forest? So young as he is, and so noble! Stand off! he will cover us all with his blood! Oh, what a groan was that! It will have broke somebody's heart-strings, I think! It would have broken mine when I was younger. But these wars make us all cruel. Yet you are worse than I am." Then again, after a pause, the patient seemed to start up in bed, and he cried out convulsively — "Give me my share, I say. Wherefore must my share be so small? There he comes past again. Now strike, now, now, now! Get his head down, my lord. He's off, by G—! Now, if he gets out of the forest, two hours will take him to Vienna. And we must go to Rome: where else could we get absolution? Oh, Heavens! the forest is full of blood, well may our hands be bloody. I see flowers all the way to Vienna: but there is blood below: oh, what a depth! what a depth! Oh! heart, heart! See how he starts up from his lair! Oh! your Highness has deceived me! There are a thousand upon one man!"

In such terms he continued to rave, until Paulina's mind was so much harassed with the constant succession of dreadful images, and frenzied ejaculations, all making report of a life passed in scenes of horror, bloodshed and violence, that at length, for her own relief, she was obliged to close the door; through which, however, at intervals, piercing shrieks or half-stifled curses still continued to find their way. It struck her as a remarkable coincidence, that something like a slender thread of connection might be found between the dreadful story narrated in the Imperial document, and the delirious ravings of this poor wretched creature, to whom accident had made her a neighbor for a single night.

Early the next morning, Paulina and her servant were summoned to resume their journey; and three hours more of rapid travelling brought them to the frowning fortress of Lovenstein. Their escort, with any one of whom they had found but few opportunities of communicating, had shown themselves throughout gloomy and obstinately silent. They knew not, therefore, to what distance their journey extended. But from the elaborate ceremonies with which they were here received, and the formal receipt for their persons, which was drawn up and delivered by the governor to the officer commanding their escort, Paulina judged that the castle of Lovenstein would prove to be their final destination.

CHAPTER XXII.

Two days elapsed without any change in Paulina's situation, as she found it arranged upon her first arrival at Lovenstein. Her rooms were not incommodious; but the massy barricades at the doors, the grated windows, and the sentinels who mounted guard upon all the avenues which led to her apartments, satisfied her sufficiently that she was a prisoner.

The third morning after her arrival brought her a still more unwelcome proof of this melancholy truth, in the summons which she received to attend a court of criminal justice on the succeeding day, connected with the tenor of its language. Her heart died within her as she found herself called upon to answer as a delinquent on a charge of treasonable conspiracy with various members of the university of Klosterheim, against the sovereign prince, the Landgrave of X——. Witnesses in exculpation, whom could she produce? Or how defend herself before a tribunal where all alike, judge, evidence, accuser, were in effect one and the same malignant enemy? In what way she could have come to be connected in the Landgrave's mind with a charge of treason against his princely rights, she found it difficult to explain, unless the mere fact of having carried the Imperial despatches in the trunks about her carriages, were sufficient to implicate her as a secret emissary or agent concerned in the Imperial diplomacy. But she strongly suspected that some deep misapprehension existed in the Landgrave's mind; and its origin, she fancied, might be found in the refined knavery of their ruffian host at Waldenhausen, in making his market of the papers which he had purloined. Bringing them forward separately and by piece-meal, he had probably hoped to receive so many separate rewards. But, as it would often happen that one paper was necessary in the way of explanation to another, and the whole, perhaps, were almost essential to the proper understanding of any one, the result would inevitably be — grievously to mislead the Landgrave. Further communications, indeed, would have tended to disabuse the Prince of any delusions raised in this way. But it was probable, as Paulina had recently learned in passing through Waldenhausen, that the ruffian's illness and delirium had put a stop to any further communication of papers; and thus the misconceptions which he had caused, were perpetuated in the Landgrave's mind.

It was on the third day after Paulina's arrival, that she was first placed before the court. The presiding officer in this tribunal was the governor of the fortress, a tried soldier, but a ruffian of low habits and cruel nature. He had risen under the Landgrave's patronage as an adventurer of desperate courage, ready for any service, however disreputable, careless alike of peril or of infamy. In common with many partisan officers, who had sprung from the ranks in this adventurous war, seeing on every side and in the highest quarters, princes as well as supreme commanders, the uttermost contempt of justice and moral principle, — he had fought his way to distinction and fortune, through every species of ignoble cruelty. He had passed from service to service, as he saw an opening for his own peculiar interest or merit, everywhere valued as a soldier of desperate enterprise, everywhere abhorred as a man. By birth a Croatian, he had exhibited himself as one of the most savage leaders of that order of barbarians in the sack of Magdeburgh, where he served under Tilly: but, latterly, he had taken service again under his original patron, the Landgrave, who had lured him back to his interest by the rank of general and the governorship of Lovestein.

This brutal officer, who had latterly lived in a state of continual intoxication, was the judge before whom the lovely and innocent Paulina was now arraigned on a charge affecting her life. In fact, it became obvious that the process was not designed for any other purpose than to save appearances, — and, if that should seem possible, to extract further discoveries from the prisoner. The general acted as supreme arbiter in every question of rights and power that arose to the court in the administration of their almost unlimited functions. Doubts he allowed of none; and cut every knot of jurisprudence, whether form or substance, by his Croatian sabre. Two assessors, however, he willingly received upon his bench of justice, to relieve him from the fatigue and difficulty of conducting a perplexed examination.

These assessors were lawyers of a low class, who tempered the exercise of their official duties with as few scruples of justice, and as little regard to the restraints of courtesy, as their military principal. The three judges were almost equally ferocious, and tools equally abject of the unprincipled sovereign whom they served.

A sovereign, however, he was; and Paulina was well aware that in his own states he had the power of life and death. She had good reason to see that her own death was resolved on; still she neglected no means of honorable self-defence. In a tone of mingled sweetness and dignity she maintained her innocence of all that was alleged against her; protested that she was unacquainted with the tenor of any papers which might have been found in her trunks; and claimed her privilege, as a subject of the Emperor, in bar of all right on the Landgrave's part to call her to account. These pleas were overruled, and when she further acquainted the court that she was a near relative of the Emperor's, and ventured to hint at the vengeance with which his Imperial Majesty would not fail to visit so bloody a contempt of justice, she was surprised to find this menace treated with mockery and laughter. In reality, the long habit of fighting for and against all the Princes of Germany, had given to the Croatian general a disregard for any of them, except on the single consideration of receiving his pay at the moment; and a single circumstance unknown to Paulina, in the final determination of the Landgrave, to earn a merit with his Swedish allies by breaking off all terms of reserve or compromise with the Imperial court, impressed a savage desperation on the tone of that Prince's policy at this particular time. The Landgrave had resolved to stake his all upon a single throw. A battle was now expected, which, if favorable to the Swedes, would lay open the road to Vienna. The Landgrave was prepared to abide the issue; not, perhaps, wholly uninfluenced to so extreme a course by the very paper which had been robbed from Paulina. His policy was known to his agents, and conspicuously influenced their manner of receiving her menace.

Menaces, they informed her, came with better grace from those who had the power to enforce them; and with a brutal scoff the Croatian bade her merit their indulgence by frank discoveries and voluntary confessions. He insisted on knowing the nature of the connection which the Imperial Colonel of Horse, Maximilian, had maintained with the students of Klosterheim; and upon other discoveries, with respect to most of which Paulina was too imperfectly informed herself to be capable of giving any light. Her earnest declarations to this effect were treated with disregard. She was dismissed for the present, but with an intimation that on the morrow she must prepare herself with a more complying temper, or with a sort of firmness in maintaining her resolution, which would not perhaps long resist those means which the law had placed at their disposal for dealing with the refractory and obstinate.

CHAPTER XXIII.

PAULINA meditated earnestly upon the import of this parting threat. The more she considered it, the less could she doubt that these fierce inquisitors had meant to threaten her with torture. She felt the whole indignity of such a threat, though she could hardly bring herself to believe them in earnest.

On the following morning she was summoned early before her judges. They had not yet assembled; but some of the lower officials were pacing up and down, exchanging unintelligible jokes, looking sometimes at herself, sometimes at an iron machine, with a complex arrangement of wheels and screws. Dark were the suspicions which assaulted Paulina as this framework, or couch of iron first met her eyes — and perhaps some of the jests circulating amongst the brutal ministers of her brutal judges would have been intelligible enough, had she condescended to turn her attention in that direction. Meantime her doubts were otherwise dispersed. The Croatian officer now entered the room alone, his assessors having probably declined participation in that part of the horrid functions which remained under the Landgrave's commission.

This man, presenting a paper with a long list of interrogatories to Paulina, bade her now rehearse verbally the sum of the answers which she designed to give. Running rapidly through them, Paulina replied with dignity, yet trembling and agitated, that these were questions which in any sense she could not answer — many of them referring to points on which she had no knowledge, and none of them being consistent with the gratitude and friendship so largely due on her side to the persons implicated in the bearing of these questions.

"Then you refuse?"

"Certainly; there are three questions only which it is in my power to answer at all — even these imperfectly. Answers such as you expect would load me with dishonor?"

"Then you refuse?"

"For the reasons I have stated, undoubtedly I do."

"Once more — you refuse?"

"I refuse, certainly; but do me the justice to record my reasons."

"Reasons! — ha! ha! they had need be strong ones if they will hold out against the arguments of this pretty plaything," laying his hand upon the machine. "However, the choice is yours, not mine."

So saying, he made a sign to the attendants. One

began to move the machine, and work the screws or raise the clanking grates and framework, with a savage din, — two others bared their arms. Paulina looked on motionless with sudden horror, and palpitating with fear.

The Croatian nodded to the men; and then in a loud commanding voice exclaimed — "The question in the first degree!"

At this moment Paulina recovered her strength, which the first panic had dispelled. She saw a man approach her with a ferocious grin of exultation. Another, with the same horrid expression of countenance, carried a large vase of water.

The whole indignity of the scene flashed full upon her mind. She, a lady of the Imperial house, threatened with torture by the base agent of a titled ruffian! She who owed him no duty — had violated no claim of hospitality, though in her own person all had been atrociously outraged!

Thoughts like these flew rapidly through her brain, when suddenly a door opened behind her. It was an attendant, with some implements for tightening or relaxing bolts. The bare-armed ruffian at this moment raised his arm to seize hers. Shrinking from the pollution of his accursed touch, Paulina turned hastily round, darted through the open door, and fled, like a dove pursued by vultures, along the passages which stretched before her. Already she felt their hot breathing upon her neck, already the foremost had raised his hand to arrest her, when a sudden turn brought her full upon a band of young women, tending upon one of superior rank, manifestly their mistress.

"Oh, madam!" exclaimed Paulina, "save me! save me!" — and with these words fell exhausted at the lady's feet.

This female — young, beautiful, and with a touching pensiveness of manners — raised her tenderly in her arms, and with a sisterly tone of affection bade her fear nothing; — and the respectful manner in which the officials retired at her command, satisfied Paulina that she stood in some very near relation to the Landgrave — in reality she soon spoke of him as her father. "Is it possible," thought Paulina to herself, "that this innocent and lovely child" (for she was not more than seventeen, though with a prematurity of womanly person that raised her to a level with Paulina's height) "should owe the affection of a daughter to a tyrant so savage as the Landgrave?"

She found, however, that the gentle Princess Adeline owed to her own childlike simplicity the best gift that one so situated could have received from the bounty of Heaven. The barbarities exercised by the Croatian governor, she charged entirely upon his own brutal nature; and so confirmed was she in this view by Paulina's own case, that she now resolved upon executing a resolution she had long projected. Her father's confidence was basely abused; this she said, and devoutly believed. "No part of the truth ever reached him; her own letters remained disregarded in a way which was irreconcilable with the testimonies of profound affection to herself, daily showered upon her by his Highness."

In reality, this sole child of the Landgrave was also the one sole jewel that gave a value in his eyes to his else desolate life. Everything in and about the castle of Lovestein was placed under her absolute control; even the brutal Croatian governor knew that no plea or extremity of circumstances would atone for one act of disobedience to her orders,—and hence it was that the ministers of this tyrant retired with so much prompt obedience to her commands.

Experience, however, had taught the Princess, that not unfrequently, orders apparently obeyed were afterwards secretly evaded; and the disregard paid of late to her letters of complaint, satisfied her that they were stifled and suppressed by the governor. Paulina, therefore, whom a few hours of unrestrained intercourse had made interesting to her heart, she would not suffer even to sleep apart from herself. Her own agitation on the poor prisoner's behalf became greater even than that of Paulina; and as fresh circumstances of suspicion daily arose in the savage governor's deportment, she now took in good earnest those measures for escape to Klosterheim which she had long arranged. In this purpose she was greatly assisted by the absolute authority which her father had conceded to her over everything but the mere military arrangements in the fortress. Under the color of an excursion, such as she had been daily accustomed to take, she found no difficulty in placing Paulina, sufficiently disguised, amongst her own servants. At a proper point of the road, Paulina and a few attendants, with the Princess herself, issued from their coaches, and bidding them await their return in half an hour's interval, by that time were far advanced upon their road to the military post of Falkenberg.

CHAPTER XXIV.

In twenty days The Mysterious Masque had summoned the Landgrave "to answer, for crimes unatoned, before a tribunal where no power but that of innocence could avail him." These days were nearly expired. The morning of the Twentieth had arrived.

There were two interpretations of this summons. By many it was believed that the tribunal contemplated was that of the Emperor; and that, by some mysterious plot, which could not be more difficult of execution than others which had actually been accomplished by The Masque, on this day the Landgrave would be carried off to Vienna. Others, again, understanding by the tribunal, in the same sense, the Imperial chamber of criminal justice, believed it possible to fulfil the summons in some way less liable to delay or uncertainty, than by a long journey to Vienna, through a country beset with enemies. But a third party, differing from both the others, understood by the tribunal where innocence was the only shield, the judgment seat of heaven; and believed on this day justice would be executed on the Landgrave, for crimes known and unknown, by a public and memorable death. Under any interpretation, however, nobody amongst the citizens could venture peremptorily to deny, after the issue of the masqued ball, and of so many other public denunciations, that The Masque would keep his word to the letter.

It followed of necessity that everybody was on the tiptoe of suspense, and that the interest hanging upon the issue of this night's events swallowed up all other anxieties, of whatsoever nature. Even the battle, which was now daily expected between the Imperial and Swedish armies, ceased to occupy the hearts and conversation of the citizens. Domestic and public concerns alike gave way to the coming catastrophe so solemnly denounced by The Masque.

The Landgrave alone maintained a gloomy reserve, and the expression of a haughty disdain. He had resolved to meet the summons with the liveliest expression of defiance, by fixing this evening for a second masqued ball, upon a greater scale than the first. In doing this he acted advisedly, and with the counsel of his Swedish allies. They represented to him that the issue of the approaching battle might be relied upon as pretty nearly certain; all the indications were indeed generally thought to promise a decisive turn in their favor; but in the worst case, no defeat of the Swedish army in this war had ever been complete; that the bulk of the retreating army, if the Swedes should be obliged to retreat, would take the road to Klosterheim, and would furnish to himself a garrison capable of holding the city for many months to come, (and *that* would not fail to bring many fresh chances to all of them,) whilst to his new and cordial allies this course would offer a secure retreat from pursuing enemies, and a satisfactory proof of his own fidelity. This even in the worst case: whereas in the better and more probable one, of a victory to the Swedes, to maintain the city but for a day or two longer against internal conspirators, and the secret co-operators outside, would be in effect to ratify any victory which the Swedes might gain by putting into their hands at a critical moment one of its most splendid trophies and guarantees.

These counsels fell too much into the Landgrave's own way of thinking to meet with any demurs from him. It was agreed, therefore, that as many Swedish troops as could at this important moment be spared, should be introduced into the halls and saloons of the castle, on the eventful evening, disguised as masquers. These were about four hundred; and other arrangements were made, equally mysterious, and some of them known only to the Landgrave.

At seven o'clock, as on the former occasion, the company began to assemble. The same rooms were thrown open; but, as the party was now far more numerous, and was made more comprehensive in point of rank, in order to include all who were involved in the conspiracy which had been some time maturing in Klosterheim, fresh suites of rooms were judged necessary, on the pretext of giving fuller effect to the princely hospitalities of the Landgrave. And, on this occasion, according to an old privilege conceded in the case of coronations or galas of magnificence, by the Lady Abbess of St. Agnes, the partition walls were removed between the great hall of the *schloss*, and the refectory of that immense convent; so that the two vast establishments, which on one side were contiguous to each other, were thus laid into one.

The company had now continued to pour in for two hours. The palace and the refectory of the convent were now overflowing with lights and splendid masques; the avenues and corridors rang with music; and, though every heart was throbbing with fear and suspense, no outward expression was wanting of joy and festal pleasure. For the present, all was calm around the slumbering volcano.

Suddenly the Count St. Aldenheim, who was standing with arms folded, and surveying the brilliant scene, felt some one touch his hand, in the way concerted amongst the conspirators as a private signal of recognition. He turned and recognized his friend, the Baron Adelort, who saluted him with three emphatic words — "We are betrayed!" — Then, after a pause, "Follow me."

St. Aldenheim made his way through the glittering crowds, and pressed after his conductor into one of the most private corridors.

"Fear not," said the other, "that we shall be watched. Vigilance is no longer necessary to our crafty enemy. He has already triumphed. Every avenue of escape is barred and secured against us: every outlet of the palace is occupied by the Landgrave's troops. Not a man of us will return alive."

"Heaven forbid we should prove ourselves such gulls! You are but jesting, my friend."

"Would to God I were! my information is but too certain. Something I have overheard by accident; something has been told me; and something I have seen. Come you also, Count, and see what I will show you: then judge for yourself."

So saying, he led St. Aldenheim by a little circuit of passages to a doorway, through which they passed into a hall of vast proportions; to judge by the catafalques, and mural monuments, scattered at intervals along the vast expanse of its walls, this seemed to be the antechapel of St. Agnes. In fact it was so; a few faint lights glimmered through the gloomy extent of this immense chamber, placed (according to the Catholic rite) at the shrine of the saint. Feeble as it was, however, the light was powerful enough to display in the centre a pile of scaffolding covered with black drapery. Standing at the foot, they could trace the outlines of a stage at the summit, fenced in with a railing, a block, and the other apparatus for the solemnity of a public execution, whilst the saw-dust below their feet ascertained the spot in which the heads were to fall.

"Shall we ascend and rehearse our parts?" asked the Count: "for methinks everything is prepared, except the headsman and the spectators. A plague on the inhospitable knave!"

"Yes, St. Aldenheim, all is prepared — even to the sufferers. On that list, you stand foremost. Believe me, I speak with knowledge; no matter where gained. It is certain."

"Well, *necessitas non habet legem;* and he that dies on Tuesday will never catch cold on Wednesday. But still, that comfort is something of the coldest. Think you that none better could be had?"

"As how?"

"Revenge, *par exemple;* a little revenge. Might one not screw the neck of this base Prince, who abuses the confidence of cavaliers so perfidiously? To die I care not; but to be caught in a trap, and die like a rat lured by a bait of toasted cheese — Faugh! my countly blood rebels against it!"

"Something might surely be done, if we could muster in any strength. That is, we might die sword in hand; but —"

"Enough! I ask no more. Now let us go. We

will separately pace the rooms, draw together as many of our party as we can single out, and then proclaim ourselves. Let each answer for one victim. I'll take his Highness for my share."

With this purpose and thus forewarned of the dreadful fate at hand, they left the gloomy ante-chapel, traversed the long suite of entertaining rooms, and collected as many as could easily be detached from the dances without too much pointing out their own motions to the attention of all present. The Count St. Aldenheim was seen rapidly explaining to them the circumstances of their dreadful situation; whilst hands uplifted, or suddenly applied to the hilt of the sword, with other gestures of sudden emotion, expressed the different impressions of rage or fear, which, under each variety of character, impressed the several hours. Some of them, however, were too unguarded in their motions; and the energy of their gesticulations had now begun to attract the attention of the company.

The Landgrave himself had his eye upon them. But at this moment his attention was drawn off by an uproar of confusion in an ante-chamber, which argued some tragical inportance in the cause that could prompt so sudden a disregard for the restraints of time and place.

CHAPTER XXV.

His Highness issued from the room in consternation, followed by many of the company. In the very centre of the ante-room, booted and spurred, bearing all the marks of extreme haste, panic, and confusion, stood a Swedish officer, dealing forth hasty fragments of some heart-shaking intelligence. "All is lost!" said he, "not a regiment has escaped!" "And the place?" exclaimed a press of inquirers. "Nordlingen." "And which way has the Swedish army retreated?" demanded a masque behind him.

"Retreat!" retorted the officer, "I tell you there *is* no retreat. All have perished. The army is no more. Horse, foot, artillery — all is wrecked, crushed, annihilated. Whatever yet lives, is in the power of the Imperialists."

At this moment the Landgrave came up, and in every way strove to check these too liberal communications. He frowned; the officer saw him not. He laid his hand on the officer's arm, but all in vain. He spoke, but the officer knew not, or forgot his rank. Panic and immeasurable sorrow had crushed his heart; he cared not for restraints; decorum and ceremony were become idle words. The Swedish army had perished. The greatest disaster of the whole Thirty Years' War had fallen upon his countrymen. His own eyes had witnessed the tragedy, and he had no power to check or restrain that which made his heart overflow.

The Landgrave retired. But in half an hour the banquet was announced; and his Highness had so much command over his own feelings, that he took his seat at the table. He seemed tranquil in the midst of general agitation; for the company were distracted by various passions. Some exulted in the great victory of the Imperialists, and the approaching liberation of Klosterheim. Some who were in the secret, anticipated with horror the coming tragedy of vengeance upon his enemies, which the Landgrave had prepared for this night. Some were filled with suspense and awe on the probable fulfilment in some way or other, doubtful as to the mode, but tragic (it was not doubted) for the result of The Masque's mysterious denunciation.

Under such circumstances of universal agitation and suspense, — for on one side or other it seemed inevitable that this night must produce a tragical catastrophe, — it was not extraordinary that silence and embarrassment should at one moment take possession of the company, and at another, that kind of forced and intermitting gayety, which still more forcibly proclaimed the trepidation which really mastered the spirits of the assemblage. The banquet was magnificent: but it moved heavily and in sadness. The music, which broke the silence at intervals, was animating and triumphant; but it had no power to disperse the gloom which hung over the evening, and which was gathering strength conspicuously as the hours advanced to midnight.

As the clock struck eleven, the orchestra had suddenly become silent; and, as no buzz of conversation succeeded, the anxiety of expectation became more painfully irritating. The whole vast assemblage was hushed, gazing at the doors — at each other — or watching, stealthily, the Landgrave's countenance. Suddenly a sound was heard in an ante-room: a page entered with a step hurried and discomposed, advanced to the Landgrave's seat, and bending downwards, whispered some news or message to that Prince, of which not a syllable could be caught by the company. Whatever were its import, it could not be collected from any very marked change on the features of him to whom it was addressed, that he participated in the emotions of the messenger, which were obviously those of grief or panic — perhaps of both united.

Some even fancied that a transient expression of malignant exultation crossed the Landgrave's countenance at this moment. But, if that were so, it was banished as suddenly; and, in the next instant, the Prince arose with a leisurely motion; and with a very successful affectation (if such it were) of extreme tranquillity, he moved forwards to one of the ante-rooms, in which, as it now appeared, some person was awaiting his presence.

Who, and on what errand? These were the questions which now racked the curiosity of those among the company who had least concern in the final event, and more painfully interested others whose fate was consciously dependent upon the accidents which the next hour might happen to bring up. Silence still continuing to prevail, and, if possible, deeper silence than before, it was inevitable that all the company — those even whose honorable temper would least have brooked any settled purpose of surprising the Landgrave's secrets — should, in some measure, become a party to what was now passing in the ante-room.

The voice of the Landgrave was heard at times — briefly and somewhat sternly in reply — but apparently in the tone of one who is thrown upon the necessity of self-defence. One the other side, the speaker was earnest, solemn, and (as it seemed) upon an office of menace or upbraiding. For a time, however, the tones were low and subdued; but, as the passion of the scene advanced, less restraint was observed on both sides; and at length many believed that in the stranger's voice they recognized that of the Lady Abbess; and it was some corroboration of this conjecture, that the name of Paulina began now frequently to be caught, and in connection with ominous words, indicating some dreadful fate supposed to have befallen her.

A few moments dispersed all doubts. The tones of bitter and angry reproach rose louder than before; they were, without doubt, those of the Abbess. She charged the blood of Paulina upon the Landgrave's head; denounced the instant vengeance of the Emperor for so great an atrocity; and, if that could be evaded, bade him expect certain retribution from Heaven for so wanton and useless an effusion of innocent blood.

The Landgrave replied in a lower key; and his words were few and rapid. That they were words of fierce recrimination was easily collected from the tone; and in the next minute the parties separated with little ceremony (as was sufficiently evident) on either side, and with mutual wrath. The Landgrave re-entered the banqueting-room — his features discomposed and inflated with passion; but such was his self-command, and so habitual his dissimulation, that, by the time he reached his seat, all traces of agitation had disappeared; his countenance had resumed its usual expression of stern serenity, and his manners their usual air of perfect self-possession.

The clock of St. Agnes struck twelve. At that sound the Landgrave rose. "Friends, and illustrious strangers!" said he, "I have caused one seat to be left empty for that blood-stained Masque who summoned me to answer on this night for a crime which he could not name, at a bar which no man knows. His summons you heard. Its fulfilment is yet to come. But I suppose few of us are weak enough to expect — "

"That The Masque of Klosterheim will ever break his engagements," said a deep voice, suddenly interrupting the Landgrave. All eyes were directed to the sound; and behold! there stood The Masque, and seated himself quietly in the chair which had been left vacant for his reception.

"It is well!" said the Landgrave; but the air of vexation and panic with which he sank back into his seat belied his words. Rising again, after a pause, with some agitation he said, "Audacious criminal! since last we met, I have learned to know you, and to appreciate your purposes. It is now fit they should be known to Klosterheim. A scene of justice awaits you at present, which will teach this city to understand the delusions which could build any part of her hopes upon yourself. Citizens and friends, not I, but these dark criminals and interlopers, whom you will presently see revealed in their true colors, are answerable for that interruption to the course of our peaceful festivities, which will presently be brought before you. Not I, but they, are responsible."

So saying, the Landgrave arose, and the whole of that immense audience, who now resumed their masques, and prepared to follow whither his Highness should lead. With the haste of one who fears he may be anticipated in his purpose, and the fury of some bird of prey, apprehending that his struggling victim may yet be torn from his talons, the Prince hurried onwards to the ante-chapel. Innumerable torches now illuminated its darkness ; in other respects it remained as St. Aldenheim had left it.

The Swedish masques had many of them withdrawn from the gala on hearing the dreadful day of Nordlingen. But enough remained, when strengthened by the body guard of the Landgrave, to make up a corps of nearly five hundred men. Under the command of Colonel Von Aremberg, part of them now enclosed the scaffold, and part prepared to seize the persons who were pointed out to them as conspirators. Amongst these stood foremost The Masque.

Shaking off those who attempted to lay hands upon

him, he strode disdainfully within the ring; and then turning to the Landgrave, he said—

"Prince, for once be generous; accept me as a ransom for the rest."

The Landgrave smiled sarcastically. "That were an unequal bargain, methinks, to take a part in exchange for the whole."

"The whole? And where is then your assurance of the whole?"

"Who should now make it doubtful? There is the block; the headsman is at hand. What hand can deliver from this extremity even you, Sir Masque?"

"That which has many times delivered me from a greater. It seems, Prince, that you forget the last days in the history of Klosterheim. He that rules by night in Klosterheim, may well expect a greater favor than this when he descends to sue for it."

The Landgrave smiled contemptuously. "But again I ask you, sir, will you on any terms grant immunity to these young men?"

"You sue as vainly for others as you would do for yourself."

"Then all grace is hopeless?" The Landgrave vouchsafed no answer, but made signals to Von Aremberg.

"Gentlemen, cavaliers, citizens of Klosterheim, you that are not involved in the Landgrave's suspicions," said The Masque appealingly, "will you not join me in the intercession I offer for these young friends, who are else to perish unjudged, by blank edict of martial law ? "

The citizens of Klosterheim interceded with ineffectual supplication. " Gentlemen, you waste your breath ; they die without reprieve," replied the Landgrave.

" Will your Highness spare none ? "

" Not one," he exclaimed angrily, " not the youngest amongst them."

" Nor grant a day's respite to him who may appear on examination the least criminal of the whole ? "

" A day's respite ? No, nor half an hour's. — Headsman, be ready. Soldiers, lay the heads of the prisoners ready for the axe."

" Detested Prince, now look to your own ! "

With a succession of passions flying over his face, rage, disdain, suspicion, the Landgrave looked round upon The Masque as he uttered these words, and with pallid, ghastly consternation, beheld him raise to his lips a hunting horn which depended from his neck. He blew a blast, which was immediately answered from within. Silence as of the grave ensued. All eyes were turned in the direction of the answer. Expectation was at its summit ; and in less than a minute solemnly uprose the curtain which divided the chapel from the ante-chapel, revealing a scene that smote many hearts with awe, and the consciences of some with as much horror as if it had really been that final tribunal, which numbers believed The Masque to have denounced.

CHAPTER XXVI.

The great chapel of St. Agnes, the immemorial hal of coronation for the Landgraves of X——, was capable of containing with ease from seven to eight thousand spectators. Nearly that number was now collected in the galleries, which, on the recurrence of that great occasion, or of a royal marriage, were usually assigned to the spectators. These were all equipped in burnished arms, the very *élite* of the Imperial army. Resistance was hopeless; in a single moment the Landgrave saw himself dispossessed of all his hopes by an overwhelming force, the advanced guard, in fact, of the victorious Imperialists, now fresh from Nordlingen.

On the marble area of the chapel, level with their own position, were arranged a brilliant staff of officers; and a little in advance of them, so as almost to reach the ante-chapel, stood the Imperial Legate or ambassador. This nobleman advanced to the crowd of Klosterheimers, and spoke thus: —

"Citizens of Klosterheim, I bring you from the Emperor your true and lawful Landgrave, Maximilian, son of your last beloved Prince."

Both chapels resounded with acclamations ; and the troops presented arms.

"Show us our Prince ! let us pay him our homage !" echoed from every mouth.

"This is mere treason !" exclaimed the Usurper. "The Emperor invites treason against his own throne, who undermines that of other Princes. The late Landgrave had no son ; so much is known to you all."

"None that was known to his murderer," replied The Masque, "else had he met no better fate than his unhappy father."

"Murderer ! And what art thou, blood-polluted Masque, with hands yet reeking from the blood of all who refused to join the conspiracy against your lawful Prince ?"

"Citizens of Klosterheim," said the Legate, "first let the Emperor's friend be assoiled from all injurious thoughts. Those whom ye believe to have been removed by murder, are here to speak for themselves."

Upon this the whole line of those who had mysteriously disappeared from Klosterheim, presented themselves to the welcome of their astonished friends.

"These," said the Legate, "quitted Klosterheim, even by the same secret passages which enabled us to enter it, and for the same-self purpose, to prepare the path for the restoration of the true heir, Maximilian the Fourth, whom in this noble Prince you behold, and whom may God long preserve!"

Saying this, to the wonder of the whole assembly he led forward The Masque, whom nobody had yet suspected for more than an agent of the true heir.

The Landgrave, meantime, thus suddenly denounced as a tyrant — usurper — murderer, had stood aloof, and had given but a slight attention to the latter words of the Legate. A race of passions had traversed his countenance, chasing each other in flying succession. But by a prodigious effort he recalled himself to the scene before him; and, striding up to the crowd, of which the Legate was the central figure, he raised his arm with a gesture of indignation, and protested vehemently that the assassination of Maximilian's father had been iniquitously charged upon himself: — "And yet," said he, "upon that one gratuitous assumption have been built all the other foul suspicions directed against my person."

"Pardon me, sir," replied the Legate, "the evidences were such as satisfied the Emperor and his Council; and he showed it by the vigilance with which he watched over the Prince Maximilian, and the anxiety with which he kept him from approaching your Highness, until his pretensions could be established by arms. But, if more direct evidence were wanting, since yesterday we have had it in the dying confession of the very agent employed to strike the fatal blow. That man died last night penitent and contrite, having fully unburdened his conscience at Waldenhausen. With evidence so overwhelming, the Emperor exacts no further sacrifice from your Highness than that of retirement from public life, to any one of your own castles in your patrimonial principality of Oberhornstein. But, now for a more pleasing duty. Citizens of Klosterheim, welcome your young Landgrave in the Emperor's name: and to-morrow you shall welcome also your future Landgravine, the lovely Countess Paulina, cousin to the Emperor, my master, and cousin also to your noble young Landgrave."

"No!" exclaimed the malignant usurper, "her you shall never see alive: for that, be well assured, I have taken care."

"Vile, unworthy Prince!" replied Maximilian, his eyes kindling with passion, "know that your intentions, so worthy of a fiend, towards that most innocent of ladies, have been confounded and brought to nothing by your own gentle daughter, worthy of a far nobler father."

"If you speak of my directions for administering the torture, a matter in which I presume that I exercised no unusual privilege amongst German sovereigns, you are right. But it was not that of which I spoke."

"Of what else then? The Lady Paulina has escaped."

"True, to Falkenberg. But, doubtless, young Landgrave, you have heard of such a thing as the intercepting of a fugitive prisoner; in such a case you know the punishment which martial law awards. The governor at Falkenberg had his orders." These last significant words he uttered in a tone of peculiar meaning. His eye sparkled with bright gleams of malice and of savage vengeance, rioting in its completion.

"Oh, heart — heart!" exclaimed Maximilian, "can this be possible?"

The Imperial Legate and all present crowded around him to suggest such consolation as they could. Some offered to ride off express to Falkenberg; some argued that the Lady Paulina had been seen within the last hour. But the hellish exulter in ruined happiness destroyed that hope as soon as it dawned: —

"Children!" said he, "foolish children! cherish not such chimeras. Me you have destroyed, Landgrave, and the prospects of my house. Now perish yourself. Look there: is that the form of one who lives and breathes?"

All present turned to the scaffold, in which direction he pointed, and now first remarked, covered with a black pall, and brought hither doubtless to aggravate the pangs of death to Maximilian, what seemed but too certainly a female corpse. The stature, the fine swell of the bust, the rich outline of the form, all pointed to the same conclusion; and in this recumbent attitude, it seemed but too clearly to present the magnificent proportions of Paulina.

There was a dead silence. Who could endure to break it? Who make the effort which was forever to fix the fate of Maximilian?

He himself could not. At last the deposed usurper, craving for the consummation of his vengeance, himself strode forward; with one savage grasp he tore away the pall, and below it lay the innocent features, sleeping in her last tranquil slumber, of his own gentle-minded daughter.

No heart was found savage enough to exult — the sorrow even of such a father was sacred. Death, and through his own orders, had struck the only being whom he had ever loved; and the petrific mace of the fell destroyer seemed to have smitten his own heart and withered its hopes forever.

Everybody comprehended the mistake in a moment. Paulina had lingered at Waldenhausen under the protection of an Imperial corps, which she had met in her flight. The tyrant, who had heard of her escape, but apprehended no necessity for such a step on the part of his daughter, had issued sudden orders to the officer commanding the military post at Falkenberg, to seize and shoot the female prisoner escaping from confinement, without allowing any explanations whatsoever, on her arrival at Falkenberg. This precaution he had adopted in part to intercept any denunciation of the Emperor's vengeance which Paulina might address to the officer. As a rude soldier, accustomed to obey the letter of his orders, this commandant had executed his commission; and the gentle Adeline, who had naturally hastened to the protection of her father's chateau, surrendered her breath meekly and with resignation to what she believed a simple act of military violence; and this she did before she could know a syllable of her father's guilt or his fall, and without any the least reason for supposing him connected with the occasion of her early death.

At this moment Paulina made her appearance unexpectedly, to reassure the young Landgrave by her presence, and to weep over her young friend, whom she had lost almost before she had come to know her. The scaffold, the corpse, and the other images of sorrow, were then withdrawn; — seven thousand Imperial troops presented arms to the youthful Landgrave and the future Landgravine, the brilliant favorites of the Emperor; — the immense area of St. Agnes resounded with the congratulations of Klosterheim; — and as the magnificent cortege moved off to the interior of the *schloss*, the swell of the Coronation anthem rising in peals upon the ear from the choir of St. Agnes, and from the military bands of the Imperial troops, awoke the promise of happier days, and of more equitable government to the long-harassed inhabitants of Klosterheim.

The Klosterheimers knew enough already, personally or by questions easily answered in every quarter, to supply any links which were wanting in the rapid explanations of the Legate. Nevertheless, that nothing might remain liable to misapprehension or cavil, a short manifesto was this night circulated by the new government, from which the following facts are abstracted : —

The last rightful Landgrave, whilst yet a young man, had been assassinated in the forest when hunting. A year or two before this catrastrophe he had contracted, what, from the circumstances, was presumed at the time, to be a *morganatic*, or left-handed marriage, with a lady of high birth, nearly connected with the Imperial House. The effect of such a marriage went to incapacitate the children who might be born under it, male or female, from succeeding. On that account, as well as because current report had represented her as childless, the widow lady escaped all attempts from the assassin. Meantime this lady, who was no other than Sister Madeline, had been thus indebted for her safety to two rumors, which were in fact equally false. She soon found means of convincing the Emperor, who had been the bosom friend of her princely husband, that her marriage was a perfect one, and conferred the fullest rights of succession upon her infant son Maximilian, whom at the earliest age, and with the utmost secrecy, she had committed to the care of his Imperial Majesty. This powerful guardian had in every way watched over the interests of the young Prince. But the Thirty Years' War had thrown all Germany into distractions, which for a time thwarted the Emperor, and favored the views of the usurper. Latterly also another question had arisen on the city and dependencies of Klosterheim as distinct from the Landgraviate. These, it was now affirmed, were a female appanage, and could only pass back to the Landgraves of X—— through a marriage with the female inheretrix. To reconcile all claims, therefore, on finding this bar in the way, the Emperor had resolved to promote a marriage for Maximilian with Paulina, who stood equally related to the Imperial house and to that of her lover. In this view he had despatched Paulina to Klosterheim, with proper documents to support the claims of both parties. Of these documents she had been robbed at Waldenhausen; and the very letter, which was designed to introduce Maximilian as "the child and sole representative of the late murdered Landgrave," falling in this surreptitious way into the usurper's hand, had naturally misdirected his attacks to the person of Paulina.

For the rest, as regarded the mysterious movements of The Masque, these were easily explained. Fear, and the exaggerations of fear, had done one-half the work to his hands — by preparing people to fall easy dupes to the plans laid, and by increasing the romantic wonders of his achievements. Co-operation also, on the part of the very students and others who stood forward as the night watch for detecting him, had served The Masque no less powerfully. The appearances of deadly struggles had been arranged artificially to countenance the plot and to aid the terror. Finally, the secret passages which communicated between the forest and the chapel of St. Agnes, (passages of which many were actually applied to that very use in the Thirty Years' War,) had been unreservedly placed at their disposal by the Lady Abbess, an early friend of the unhappy Landgravine, who sympathized deeply with that lady's unmerited sufferings.

One other explanation followed, communicated in a letter from Maximilian to the Legate; this related to the murder of the old seneschal, a matter in which the young Prince took some blame to himself — as having unintentionally drawn upon that excellent servant his unhappy fate. "The seneschal," said the writer, "was the faithful friend of my family, and knew the whole course of its misfortunes. He continued his abode at the *schloss*, to serve my interest; and in some measure I may fear that I drew upon him his fate. Traversing late one evening a suite of rooms, which his assistance and my own mysterious disguise laid open to my passage at all hours, I came suddenly upon the Prince's retirement. He pursued me, but with hesitation: some check I gave to his motions by halting before a portrait of my unhappy father, and emphatically pointing his attention to it. Conscience, I well knew, would supply a commentary to my act. I produced the impression which I had anticipated, but not so strongly as to stop his pursuit. My course necessarily drew him into the seneschal's room. The old man was sleeping; and this accident threw into the Prince's hands a paper, which, I have reason to think, shed some considerable light upon my own pretensions, and, in fact, first made my enemy acquainted with my existence and my claims. Meantime, the seneschal had secured the Prince's vengeance upon himself. He was now known as a faithful agent in my service. That fact signed his death-warrant. There is a window in a gallery which commands the interior of the seneschal's room. On the evening of the last *fête*, waiting there for an opportunity of speaking securely with this faithful servant, I heard a deep groan, and then another, and another; I raised myself, and with an ejaculation of horror, looked down upon the murderer — then surveying his victim with hellish triumph. My loud exclamation drew the murderer's eye upwards: under the pangs of an agitated conscience, I have reason to think that he took me for my unhappy father, who perished at my age, and is said to have resembled me closely. Who that murderer was, I need not say more directly. He fled with the terror of one who flies from an apparition. Taking a lesson from this incident, on that same night, by the very same sudden revelation of what passed, no doubt, for my father's countenance, aided by my mysterious character, and the proof I had announced to him immediately before of my acquaintance with the secret of the seneschal's murder — in this and no other way it was, that I produced that powerful impression upon the Prince which terminated the festivities of that evening, and which all Klosterheim witnessed. If not, it is for the Prince to explain in what other way I did or could affect him so powerfully."

This explanation of the else unaccountable horror manifested by the Ex-Landgrave on the sudden exposure of The Masque's features, received a remarkable confirmation from the confession of the miserable assassin at Waldenhausen. This man's illness had been first brought on by the sudden shock of a situation pretty nearly the same, acting on a conscience more disturbed and a more superstitious mind. In the very act of attempting to assassinate or rob Maximilian, he had been suddenly dragged by that Prince into a dazzling light; and this settling full upon features which too vividly recalled to the murderer's recollection the last unhappy Landgrave, at the very same period of blooming manhood, and in his own favorite hunting palace, not far from which the murder had been perpetrated, naturally enough had for a time unsettled the guilty man's understanding, and terminating in a nervous fever, had at length produced his penitential death.

A death, happily of the same character, soon overtook the deposed Landgrave. He was laid by the side of his daughter, whose memory, as much even as his own penitence, availed to gather round his final resting-place the forgiving thoughts even of those who had suffered most from his crimes. Klosterheim in the next age flourished greatly, being one of those cities which benefited by the peace of Westphalia. Many changes took place in consequence, greatly affecting the architectural character of the town and its picturesque antiquities; but, amidst all revolutions of this nature, the secret passages still survive, and to this day are shown occasionally to strangers of rank and consideration, by which, more than by any other of the advantages at his disposal, The Masque of Klosterheim was enabled to replace himself in his patrimonial rights, and at the same time to liberate from a growing oppression his own compatriots and subjects.

www.ingramcontent.com/pod-product-compliance
Lightning Source LLC
LaVergne TN
LVHW010229110826
845151LV00004B/1232
* 9 7 8 1 4 2 5 5 2 5 8 5 9 *